A Candlelight Ecstasy Romance™

"DO YOU WANT ME TO TREAT YOU LIKE A WOMAN?"

Charly's undoing was her next challenge, and she knew it the minute she uttered the words. "I don't think you know how. You've been away from a woman for a long time!"

"Not as long as you think. I haven't claimed celibacy yet." In one swift movement he stood, encircled her in his arms, and kissed her with such skillful fervor that Charly clung weakly to his back. Her heart beat rapidly and she responded to his demanding lips in spite of herself. She was unable to resist, unwilling to stop him. A soft moan escaped her. In another moment she was lost to this ruffian she barely knew . . .

CANDLELIGHT ECSTASY ROMANCES™

CAPTIVE DESIRE

Tate McKenna

A CANDLELIGHT ECSTASY ROMANCE™

To Roger, who never doubted me; and Mary Lynn, who was midwife to this birth.

Published by
Dell Publishing Co., Inc.
1 Dag Hammarskjold Plaza
New York, New York 10017

Dell ® TM 681510, Dell Publishing Co., Inc.

Candlelight Ecstasy Romance™ is a trademark of
Dell Publishing Co., Inc., New York, New York.

ISBN: 0-440-11238-9

Printed in the United States of America

First printing—August 1982

To Our Readers:

We have been delighted with your enthusiastic response to Candlelight Ecstasy Romances™ and we thank you for the interest you have shown in this exciting series.

In the upcoming months, we will continue to present the distinctive, sensuous love stories you have come to expect only from Ecstasy. We look forward to bringing you many more books from your favorite authors and also the very finest work from new authors of contemporary romantic fiction.

As always, we are striving to present the unique, absorbing love stories that you enjoy most—books that are more than ordinary romance.

Your suggestions and comments are always welcome. Please write to us at the address below.

Sincerely,

Anne Gisonny
Senior Editor
Candlelight Romances

CHAPTER ONE

The car lunged backwards, tilting to the back right corner. Charly pressed the accelerator, but the vehicle refused to move, and she heard a dragging sound. She hopped out quickly, fearing the car had sunk into one of those ruts. Charly stared long seconds at the limp tire, then kicked it angrily.

"A flat! Out here in the middle of nowhere!" she wailed aloud. Her irritated voice echoed from the towering pines and thick oaks and through the Tennessee mountain air. Then there was a quiet stillness, and all she could hear was water rushing in the stream that ran parallel to the rutted road. "Damn!" she muttered, stalking back to the open car door to turn off the ignition.

The discreet rustling of dry leaves attracted her attention and Charly looked up apprehensively. Seeing nothing, she whirled around, brown eyes searching frantically through the thick summer-green foliage. A clatter from above caused her to crane her neck. There, sitting arrogantly on a tree limb, was a bushy squirrel, his furry tail curled behind his back. He fussed at her in rapid-fire chatter, then scampered away.

"Whew!" breathed Charly, relief flooding over her. Haunting visions of the movie *Deliverance* sent a chilling shiver through her slim frame. For a moment she imagined someone hiding in the leaves, watching her. She

9

managed a little laugh at her apprehension. Still, it was awfully quiet.

At least I can change a tire, she thought bitterly. So I may as well get to it. There is no one out here to help me . . . except that stupid squirrel.

Charly secured the emergency brake, then opened up the trunk. Pulling with all her might on the spare tire, she dragged it out of the car, letting it bounce and flop on the ground. She fumbled with the jack, fitting it together and pushing it under the sunken fender. A furious pumping motion impelled the jack to work and it began to raise the rear of the small compact car. Then, moving around to the deflated tire, she pried around the hub cap. It popped off and clattered across the rocks.

"Damn! A fingernail!" Charly muttered, grabbing her stricken finger. The nail had been ripped off, tearing into the tender skin beneath. It began to throb, and blood oozed slowly around the painful nail.

Abruptly, distant dead leaves rustled again, this time accompanied by the distinct crack of a dry stick. Fearfully, Charly froze in a half-bending position, holding her injured finger. The noise was approaching, getting louder. Someone—or something—was definitely coming toward Charly!

The ponderous silence was rent by the resonant sound of a male voice. "Are you all right?"

Charly whirled around to face him, brown eyes wide with fright, heart pounding loudly in her ears.

"Well, are you? Do you need help?" He motioned toward the car.

Charly could only stare, speechless, at the rugged man who had emerged from the woods. She took a step backwards, preparing to run. Possibly she could lock herself in her car until help came. But *what* help? Panicky fear gripped her, and she completely forgot about the injured

10

finger, which by now dripped small spots of blood to the rocks beside her feet.

"What happened?" He motioned to the bleeding finger and started toward her.

"N-nothing. It's—it's just a broken fingernail. It's all r-right," Charly stammered hoarsely, taking another step backwards.

The man stood over six feet tall and was dressed in faded jeans, a well-worn tan sport shirt, and scuffy shoes. He seemed overpowering, for his dark hair dominated his appearance. Only intense blue eyes were visible beneath the shaggy, black hair that hung over his forehead and framed his entire jawline. The rich sable beard and thick hair framed his craggy features and accented his lean, muscular body. There was a light scattering of dark hair on both corded forearms, ending with small inky patches on each long finger. Charly shuddered involuntarily, fearing that her worst nightmares had suddenly appeared before her in an almost macabre reality. Tales of mountain men flashed through her wildly racing mind, and she wondered recklessly if she could possibly outrun him. Charly couldn't shake the terror that gripped her as the man's all-encompassing gaze flowed from her to the car and back again.

"Do you want me to change your tire?" His voice was a low rumble.

Charly froze, not knowing whether to accept his help or run for her life.

He spread his hands toward her and claimed, "I won't hurt you, lady. I'll just help you with this tire so you can be on your way."

As he spoke, Charly's confidence grew slightly. He was obviously educated and somewhat refined in his manner and . . . there was something in those daring blue eyes that reflected a spark of credibility. Actually, if he was willing to change the tire, perhaps she should accept his aid. He seemed sincere.

"Okay," she said haltingly. Honestly, she didn't have much choice.

Charly stayed near the car door apprehensively as he bent to the job. The man reached for the discarded tool and finished loosening the bolts that attached the tire to the car, working rapidly with skillful, precise hands. He grunted softly as he lifted the heavy tire from the hub, then looked inquisitively at Charly. "What are you doing up here by yourself?" he asked.

"I'm . . . I'm here on business," Charly admitted.

He furrowed ebony eyebrows as he continued working, never looking up at her. "Business? What business could you possibly have way up here?"

Charly pursed her lips thoughtfully. Just how much should she tell this stranger? "I'm here to meet someone. What are you doing up here in this wilderness?" She could play the question game, too.

He lifted the spare tire and slid it onto the axle, his muscular arms bulging with the strain. "Hand me that tire tool, will you?" he directed Charly.

Reluctantly, she handed it to him. As her hesitant brown eyes met his sharp blue ones, he answered, "I was fishing when I heard your noise." His rough hand graced hers as he took the cold metal tool.

Charly watched silently as he tightened the nuts that secured the tire until they squeaked. She pondered the credibility of his explanation. Fishing? Yet she knew that there were trout streams nearby and many people came into the national park to fish. It sounded reasonable. Still, the stranger had appeared mysteriously. Could she trust anyone who looked as rugged as he did? Undeniably, she was a little awed by him. He had been nice enough to fix her tire. And underneath that shaggy appearance, she suspected, was a reasonably handsome man. His eyes certainly held an arresting appeal.

With a heaving grunt, he lifted the flat tire into the trunk along with the tools. Then, turning to face her, he directed assertively, "There is a widening of the road up ahead by that curve. You can use it to turn around." He slammed the trunk, punctuating his decisive remark.

Charly eyed him defiantly. "Oh, I'm not turning around. I am going on to the end of this road. But, thanks for changing my tire, Mr. . . . uh . . . what is your name?"

The man's dark brows came together in a frown. He looked at her for long moments, carefully assessing the chestnut hair piled on her uplifted head, the slim neck, the high breasts hidden behind a white cotton blouse. His arrogant eyes continued down her frame, taking in her slender hips, long straight legs, and ending with the smart, wedge-heeled shoes that revealed neat pink-nailed toes. His lips thinned with contempt and his voice was unrelentingly hard. "The person you are meeting couldn't possibly be up here. This road isn't open to the public. It doesn't go anywhere of interest."

"Oh, yes it does," Charly disputed stoutly. "It leads to Walter Simms's house. And if you're through stripping me, I'll be on my way." Her brown eyes flashed and she flung open her car door. She crawled into the small car and grabbed a tissue, wrapping it around her injured finger.

Although the bleeding had stopped, it throbbed uncomfortably. By the time she looked back up, the bearded stranger was gone. He had vanished completely. Charly looked around, overcome with an eerie feeling. Where had he gone? And why had he disappeared so quickly? How strange . . .

She shrugged and started the car, proceeding on her journey up the rugged mountain road. She glanced at her gold watch. Had it only been two hours since her small compact car had rolled to a stop at the forest ranger's house? Somehow it seemed much longer as she reflected on her meeting with the ranger, who had directed her to this remote area. He had issued warnings and offered to accompany her. Now why had she refused?

The screen door had creaked as a tall uniformed man emerged from the house and stood in greeting on the roofed porch. "Howdy." He waved one hand, then rested it on a nearby post while Charly made her way to the ranger's house.

"Hello," she answered with a friendly smile. "I'm Charly Ryan, from the Bureau of Land Management's regional office. Did you get my letter?" She squinted in the bright Tennessee sunlight, shading her brown eyes.

The man's crinkled smile faded to a solemn acknowledgment. "Yes, ma'am. I got your letter last week. But from the name I expected . . . well, I didn't expect a girl."

Charly smiled good-naturedly. "I always get some reaction to my name. Actually, it's short for Charlene, compliments of my younger brother."

"I see," he responded, scrutinizing her trim form. "Did you drive all the way from Atlanta?"

She shook her head. "I flew to Knoxville, then drove over here yesterday. I'm staying at The Azalea Inn until my business here is finished." Charly's voice couldn't hide her annoyance at having to rent a car and drive the hundred miles from Knoxville. The small town she sought was nestled in the mountains on the border of North Carolina and Tennessee, far from airports and, in Charly's opinion, conveniences. But she was determined to make the best of it. After all, sometimes inconveniences came with the job in order to prove flexibility in any situation. And it was Charly's intent to prove her flexibility, as well as her ability, with no complaints.

The man raised his graying eyebrows at her words, as

14

if he read more into them. "Would you like to come in for a glass of tea?" he asked kindly.

"No, thank you." Charly declined, tucking a loose strand of chestnut hair back into the neat twist where she had piled her thick curls in an effort to get some relief from the humid late-August heat. "I just stopped by to report in and find out how to reach Walter Simms. I tried to find his number in the phone book, but he isn't listed."

The ranger ran his hand over his face, briefly smoothing out the wrinkled cheeks. "Well, now, the only way you're going to see Walter Simms is to go after him. He lives up on the mountain. And there's no phone." He waved his thick-veined hand toward the green and yellow mound rising high behind them.

"That's fine. Just tell me how to get there, Mr. . . . uh . . ." Her eyes traveled down to the metal nametag attached to his uniform pocket. " . . . Crockett."

"Are you sure you want to go all the way up there? It won't do you any good, I can tell you right now."

Charly drew herself up, trying to elevate to his tall frame. But there was no way to stretch her five-feet, four-inch length to match his six-feet, two or three. Arrogantly, she looked up at him and said, "Let me worry about that. All I need is directions to his house."

Crockett's eyebrows furrowed, and his eyes took on a friendly glow as he drawled, "I'm not very busy today. Would you like for me to take you up there? It's a long distance."

Confidently, she declined his offer. "No, thank you. Just give me directions and I'll be on my way." It was obvious that the ranger didn't think she could manage this trip alone. However, she had dealt with his typical male attitude before and just humored him patiently.

"Well, I guess that's how a girl like you got such an important big-city job. You're spunky, aren't you?" His gray eyes twinkled as his face softened slightly.

Charly couldn't help smiling at his old-fashioned adjective describing her. Actually, his assessment seemed fairly accurate. She had to be *spunky* to make it in the man's world in which she worked. She considered herself equal to any of her co-workers—even her boss, Lewis Daniel. Maybe her attitude was "spunky" after all. *Tough* was the word Lewis had used.

"I'm just doing my job, Mr. Crockett. Which way to Mr. Simms's?"

The tall ranger motioned toward the road and, unavoidably, the mountain. "Well, now, you just follow this road all the way to the top. It's about thirty miles. When the blacktop road ends, you'll cross a bridge, then go on another half-mile on the graveled part. You'll see the dirt road that takes you to the left, up Simms Hollow. It follows Little Creek all the way up to ol' Walt's cabin, about five miles. By then you'll cross the state line and be in North Carolina."

Charly nodded briskly at his directions, given in his slow Southern drawl. "Thirty-five miles. That's not so bad, especially after the trip I just made from Knoxville." She felt reassured that the man she sought was so close.

"It's a slow-paced drive. And the last five will be the longest. That road's pretty rough."

"Thanks for the directions, Mr. Crockett." Charly turned to go, then looked back with a smile. She was in the Smoky Mountains, and it was just too much of a coincidence to pass. "You aren't related to *Davy* Crockett, are you?"

He grinned, revealing furrowed crow's-feet around his gray eyes. "I always get comments about my name, too," he quipped. "Ol' Davy was from Cumberland way, not the Smokies. But you never know—maybe one of his sons roamed over this way, leaving his kin in these mountains."

Charly's eyes twinkled at the ranger's suggestive com-

16

ment. "It might be interesting to research your roots, Mr. Crockett. Thanks for the directions."

"Sure thing. Drive carefully and . . . oh, Miss Ryan . . ."

Charly glanced up from the car door.

"Watch out for the weather. Don't get stuck up in Simms Hollow if it rains." He pointed toward the sky, where faintly gray-edged clouds dotted the blue expanse. "Looks like we could get rain before the day's over."

"Okay." Charly nodded, immediately forgetting his warning. She backed out of the driveway and headed for the curvy mountain road that led to her destination. The sky was mostly blue, and the sun beat down unmercifully as she drove away from the sleepy little Tennessee town.

She left the farms and stretches of fields that nestled at the foot of the mountains and immediately started winding her way upward into the elevated forests. A brown wooden sign announced her entrance into the Great Smoky Mountains National Forest and she sped onward. Humid air from the open windows swirled around her, loosening short hair around her neckline. It was a good feeling and the beauty of the scenery raised her spirits.

She flipped on her car radio, and the only station that penetrated the deep recesses of her remote location was a country music station. With singular guitar accompaniment, a man sang in sad tones about Smoky Mountain rain and his lost love. However, the woeful notes contrasted with Charly's buoyant mood, and she switched it off again, humming her own happy tune.

She mused over her conversation with Mr. Crockett, possible distant relative of the eminent Davy. He had called her "spunky." In such a remote region as this, he probably hadn't seen many women who held positions of influence, especially in government. Charly prided herself on her job and her ability to carry out proposals and make decisions. She would show Lewis Daniel that she could

17

complete this assignment, however unpleasant. He had expressed some doubts about her ability to do it. As her boss, he had even suggested that she take the assistant regional manager with her. But she would show him! She could handle these backwoods people and accomplish her goal—with their endorsement. He'd see.

The trip turned out to be slower than she had anticipated. The further she went, the more narrow and winding the road became. Charly found that she couldn't speed around the mountainous curves and was forced to take them slowly. Eventually she decided to make it a relaxing trip and enjoy her surroundings. She even stopped several times to view the spectacular mountain scenery.

Charly watched in awe as white frothy water cascaded over Bald River Falls, emitting a fine mist spray that glittered in the morning sunlight. The water pelted downward, finally rushing loudly beneath the bridge where Charly stood. From there it slowed its pace and washed over rust and gray rocks, lingering in the deeper pools.

She had studied maps of the area and knew that this large river was fed by numerous smaller tributaries that ran down from the mountaintops. Little Creek, where Walter Simms lived, was one of those tributaries. Breathing in the cool, moist air, Charly felt very close to nature as she continued her trek into the interior of the southern Appalachian range.

Her quest for the home of Walter Simms had led to this secluded road and, ultimately, the flat tire and the mysterious mountaineer. When would she reach the end of her journey? The rutted road jolted her to the present.

Finally, Charly could see a clearing ahead. Thank goodness she had reached the end of the road. What a nerve-wracking trip it had been. She tried to dismiss the strange, bearded mountain man who had helped her, then disappeared so suddenly. But his relentless blue eyes and rough appearance remained with her, even though she had not learned his name.

Charly emerged from the dark tree-shaded road into a bath of sunshine and spotted a weathered cabin nestled against the side of the mountain almost hidden by the trees. She parked near an old yellow truck of 1950 vintage and walked around to the steps that led to the high porch, where a man stood. He watched her every move. She noted that he must be the sought-after Walter Simms.

She took a deep, confidence-building breath and smiled. "Hello. I'm Charly Ryan. Are you Walter Simms?" She gazed at the stoop-shouldered man and marveled at the eighty-nine-year-old countenance before her.

"Howdy," he answered in a creaky voice. "Yep, I'm Walter Simms. Y'say your name's 'Charly'? Funny name for a girl." He shuffled over to a wood-slat rocker and gestured for her to sit down. "Come on and join me. I was just about to have some lunch. Would you like some, and a glass of tea?"

Charly smiled in acceptance. "Tea sounds great, Mr. Simms. Let me help you."

"No, you have a seat. I can do it." He stepped into the house, leaving Charly alone on the porch.

She could see a small barn, the nearest wall of which was lined with stretched-out raccoon skins. She shuddered at the thought of the little masked animals. Slumping into the wooden rocker, Charly was surprised at how comfortable it was—or maybe she was just tired from the oppressive humidity and her long hours in the car during the last two days. There was a peaceful yawn in the air, punctuated only by the buzz of flies gathering in the heat of the day. The sound of the screen door shooed them away and alerted Charly that Mr. Simms was returning.

He set a platter piled with tomato wedges, cheese slices, and crackers on a table between them and handed her a tall glass of tea that was graced with a green mint leaf.

Gratefully, Charly gulped the cool liquid, then set the glass on the table, watching the pungent mint leaf float languidly to the bottom of the glass. They ate the simple food quietly for a few minutes before Charly broke the silence.

"Mr. Simms, I'm from the Bureau of Land Management in Atlanta. That's the organization that oversees the use of this government land." She motioned toward the surrounding hills.

He nodded and reached for a wedge of tomato. "The government?"

She watched him manage the juicy tomato without so much as a dribble. "Yes, sir. The government."

His lively blue eyes caught hers. "What do you want with me?"

"I . . . I came to see . . . to check on the proper use of this land." She would not be intimidated by this man. She came up here for a reason and she would not back down. Reaching for a piece of pale yellow cheese, she bit into it.

"Is that all? Well, I can show you that right quick. Come on," he said enthusiastically. He reached for a cheese wedge and placed it on a cracker before leading the way down the steps to the yard.

She followed the spry old man, hurrying to keep up with him.

"Here's my garden. I have to work all the time to keep the deer and rabbits from eating the whole thing." He pointed to the ample plot of ground, tilled and completely fenced in. There wasn't a weed around any of the plants and Charly was amazed that, at his age, Walter Simms could prepare such a beautiful garden and coax so many vegetables to grow. The garden would go into her official report.

They walked past the barn with its covering of raccoon skins. Irritated at the gruesome sight, Charly remarked, "Mr. Simms, don't you know that killing animals in a national forest is against federal regulations?" Raccoon skins would certainly be included in the report.

He stopped and flashed his blue eyes at her. "I've been huntin' 'coons all my life, lady, and I'm not gonna quit now." After a pause, he added quickly, "Besides, I killed them on my own property."

"Still, Mr. Simms, these animals belong to the forest. How could you possibly kill them?"

"Survival. It's all survival. I only take what I can use. And I'm surviving in the forest, too." He turned and led her to a row of perfectly square white boxes.

As they approached, she could hear the buzzing and knew their purpose. "Bee hives!" she exclaimed in recognition.

"Yep," he nodded proudly. "They keep me in honey all year and I still have some to sell and trade. There's basswood, poplar, and sourwood trees all around here and my bees produce the best honey you'll find anywhere."

Charly watched in awe as he opened one of the drawers and casually brushed aside a small group of bees with his bare hands.

"Here, taste this." He pinched off a small portion of the honeycomb with its sweet filling. "Put the whole thing in your mouth. That 'comb' won't hurt you. It's just wax . . . beeswax . . . hee-hee." His laughter was high and slightly squeaky.

Charly obeyed and popped the entire thing in her mouth, chewing on the wax while the marvelous sweet honey oozed onto her tongue. She continued to chew on the wax until it was a small, tough ball. The bees, too, would be a part of the report. Following Walter Simms back to the house, she tried to prepare him for what she had to say.

"Mr. Simms, don't you miss civilization way up here all by yourself?"

"Nope. People just get in my way."

21

"But you must get lonesome sometimes."

"I'm too busy to get lonesome. I'm getting ready for winter right now."

"Winter?" Charly made a mental note, for here was another tactic she could use in the report. "The winters up here must be awful. How do you get to town for supplies?"

"I don't." He climbed the steps, holding on to the gray weathered railing with a gnarled hand.

"You can't get down for supplies?" she asked incredulously. Another item for the report.

"Nope. Snow's too deep." He paused at the top step to catch his breath.

"Then what do you do? It's dangerous for you to be up here like that."

"That's why I get ready for winter. I store up firewood, supplies, food—everything I'll need for the winter months. Then I don't worry about it." He sat in his straight-backed rocker and looked peacefully over the land.

"Mr. Simms, as a representative of the government, I have made an assessment of this land and the best use of it. I am also concerned about your welfare. Therefore, I would like to make a proposal. We will pay you for your land, your house—everything here. We will help you to relocate down in town where you'll be closer to friends, supplies, and medical facilities. It'll be for your own good."

"Hold on, young lady!" Alarm filled Simms's cracked voice. "I have a lifetime lease—from the government—that says I can stay here until I die. Then"—and he shook a crooked finger at Charly—"and, *only then* can the government come in here and take over my land."

Charly nodded. "Yes, I know about your lifetime lease. And we will uphold it. But you are abusing the land. You are killing raccoons, plowing up the land, depleting this area of its wildlife."

22

He hit the flat of his thick sturdy hand on the chair arm, making a loud *spat.* "I'm *not* depleting this land! I'm just living here! It's survival of the fittest! Haven't you ever heard of that?"

"Yes, but this is now protected public domain. Federal laws protect the land and animals, trying to save them for the next generations." Charly knew her explanations sounded feeble to this stubborn old man.

"This is *my* land! What about *me?* What about this generation . . . *this* old man?" He poked himself on the chest for emphasis.

"Believe me, we are concerned about you, Mr. Simms. That's why we want you to move to town. Then you can be closer to people who can care for you—your family, friends, doctors."

"I don't need anybody to take care of me. And I don't have much use for doctors. I've got my own remedies from the mountain. I'm staying right here. I won't let anybody drive me off my land."

Charly smiled. "I'm not trying to drive you off your land. I'm only trying to help you."

"Help me? The government? Huh!" He looked away disgustedly. Abruptly he stood up, gesturing in the air as he spoke. "I've lived on this mountain for over sixty years and never asked for help from the government or anybody! And I don't intend to start now. I won't let you drive me from my land!" With that, he stomped angrily inside the house, letting the screen door bang loudly.

Charly blinked, feeling a little sorry for the old man, who embodied such bitterness. Although his words to her were harsh, she understood his deep feelings about the land. It didn't make her job any easier. She knew what her boss, Lewis, wanted—had demanded. Sighing, she rose. She knew it was futile to continue today, for her visit with Walter Simms had come to an end. She would return to town and give him some time to cool off, but she wouldn't admit defeat yet. The initial report could be filed while she regathered her forces. She might have to consult with Lewis after all.

As Charly reached her car, the oppressive humidity closed in on her. Flies buzzed near her head and she swung her hand to shoo them away just as the first large raindrops started to fall. She hadn't noticed that the dark-edged clouds had covered the blue sky and cast a gray shadow over the afternoon. Now huge wet drops bounced on the dusty car, plopped on the dry earth, and ran over her arms before Charly could jump into the dry shelter of the car. She sat for a moment in silence, listening to the rain as it pelted the car, recalling the ranger's warning not to get caught in the rain in Simms Hollow. Well, thank goodness she was leaving just in time. She started the motor, drowning out the soft patter of a million raindrops hitting the roof and windows.

When she reached the dirt road, she plunged swiftly ahead, dodging ruts and large rocks. The rain had turned the road into a soggy path where her car slid and skidded its way along the muddy rivulets. Charly leaned forward, straining to see through the gray haze caused by the severity of the sudden downpour.

Charly had traveled about a mile down the slippery road when she felt the car swerve. She struggled with the steering wheel, wrestling impotently to control her vehicle until, at last, she felt the helpless swing of the car out of control as it slid first one way, then the other. Finally, after what seemed like a slow-motion eternity, the car slumped securely to a dead halt. Fear knotted in the pit of her stomach as the little car tilted threateningly on one side, sinking even further into the mud. She worked feverishly to open the door, but it was wedged shut against grass and mud, which were closely visible outside her window. She struggled over to the passenger side of the car and opened that door, climbing out into the driving rain. She assessed

24

the extent of the damage, eyeing the little car, which leaned precariously on its side in a water-filled ditch next to the mud-slick road. As the wind blew swirls of wet leaves against her and cold rain sent chilly streams of water down her back, Charly knew that it would be risky to crawl back into the small compact car with it so dangerously tilted.

Consequently, she reached inside and grabbed her purse and locked the door securely, leaving her scattered portfolio in the back seat.

The wind was cold and Charly was immediately drenched from head to toe as she stood stewing over her predicament. There was only one thing to do. She would have to go back to Walter Simms's cabin and wait out the storm. She dreaded the thought of facing him again, but there was no alternative. The car was stuck—and so was she.

Charly started hiking through the mud, her stylish, wedge-heeled shoes proving to be impossible for clomping through the mud. The only reason she left them on was to protect herself from the rocks, for she had to stop periodically to scrape thick mud from the sides and bottoms. As she trudged through the cold rain, darkness closed in. The rain was steady and hard, and occasionally the gray-black forest blazed with the flash of lightning or echoed with the rumble of distant thunder.

Charly was chilled thoroughly, teeth chattering, hands and arms shaking, and legs almost rubber from fear and cold. How could it be so cold when only a few hours ago the heat had been oppressive? The ranger, Crockett, had been right when he predicted rain. And she should never have come up the mountain alone. Suddenly, an additional fear gripped Charly. She remembered the bearded man who had appeared and disappeared so suddenly in the forest! What if . . . ? But she refused to think of it. Frantically, for more than an hour, Charly struggled on up the road to the security of the old man's cabin. She tried not to imagine what might be behind every tree and bush.

She moved faster, almost running up the road, fearfully looking over her shoulder every few minutes. What if he was watching her, stalking her? Every time the lightning flashed she took advantage of the light by searching through her pitch-black surroundings. The storm, the cold rain, the random lightning were no longer her enemies. *He* was—whoever was out there!

Whatever had convinced her to come to this remote, uncivilized place by herself anyway? She should never have let Lewis . . . but he tried to tell her. Damn him! He should have insisted. But would she have listened? Probably not. Next time . . . if there *was* a next time! Oh—what a terrible thought.

It seemed forever before she spotted a weak light shining from the distant cabin, beaming warmth and comfort out into the cold, miserably wet night. Breathlessly, she ran to the house, slipping out of her ruined shoes, leaving them on the bottom step in the rain. She stumbled clumsily onto the porch and knocked loudly at the door. Her voice rose to a wailful, rather frantic, "Mr. Simms, Mr. Simms! It's me, Charly Ryan!"

Walter Simms opened the door slowly and stared at Charly. What a mess she was. What a dripping, shivering, muddy mess! But, thank goodness, she was safe!

Her chestnut hair was torn from its chic twist and hung drooping over her shoulders. Her face was streaked and mascara smudged into two inky blotches beneath her eyes. Her white blouse clung wetly to her body, outlining her breasts and heaving ribs. The once-clean gray slacks were mud-speckled and wrapped tightly around her thighs. And her bare feet were covered with brown oozing mud.

"M-Mr. Simms, I had car trouble," she muttered through chattering teeth. "C-Can I . . . come in?"

He looked at her for a long minute, assessing the young

girl in his old, slow way. He rubbed a gnarled hand over his rough chin stubble. Finally, when she thought he would never answer, he said, "Guess I don't have a choice. You don't have any other place to go." He stepped aside. "Come on in."

Charly stepped gratefully into the warm room, which glowed with the flames from a huge fireplace. The welcoming blaze enticed Charly and she was drawn involuntarily toward it.

Abruptly, she stopped short, a muffled cry in her throat. There, kneeling before the fire and placing logs in a certain neat order, was the dark, foreboding form of a large man. He swung his head around to look at her and the fire's glow lit his shadowed face, revealing the same bearded fisherman who had changed her tire earlier that day! Charly gasped, fear rising within her once again. Just when she thought she had reached safe harbor, her sanctuary in the mountains was invaded by the menacing figure before her. She sought refuge in the cabin with the very man from whom she was trying to escape! And she was trapped miles from civilization and no chance of help from anyone except old Walter Simms!

CHAPTER TWO

"What are you doing here?" Charly questioned disdainfully.

The dark man's steely eyes raked over her drenched, accentuated curves as he answered, "It happens to be where I live. What are *you* doing here?"

Charly was all too aware of her wet, suggestive appearance. She crossed her arms to hide her breasts from this stranger, whose eyes chilled her. She clutched both forearms. It made her realize just how cold she really was. "You live here? This is Walter Simms's house. I thought he lived alone. Who are you?"

The man turned away from her indifferently and continued to complete his task with the fire. Ignoring her question, he asked his own. "Who are you, and what in the hell are you doing here at this time of night?"

"I'm . . . I'm Charly Ryan. My car is stuck in the mud about two miles down the road. I had to leave it there and walk back here through the rain. Do you think you could help me get it out?"

"Tonight? No way! Looks like you're stranded. What is your business up here?"

Charly wasn't sure why she felt compelled to tell this stranger about herself, but she did. Maybe it was his overpoweringly dominant attitude or his gruff appearance. Maybe it was just his indifference as he turned his broad back to her.

"I'm from the B.L.M.—the Bureau of Land Management—and I'm here on assignment. When I came up here earlier today, I didn't notice the impending storm. Now that road is just awful. Once my car started sliding, I couldn't control it."

"So you want to spend the night," he finished, as a statement of fact.

"No, I don't *want* to, but I guess I have no choice," Charly snipped, hugging her arms around her, trying to warm her chilled body. She shivered visibly just as he looked back at her and she cringed under his all-consuming gaze. "Unless, of course, there is a motel nearby!"

Once again, his eyes traveled down her, ending with her muddy feet and the growing pool of water gathering on the floor around her. He stood up and his dark presence significantly dominated the room.

"Come over here closer to the fire and I'll get you a towel." His voice was a sharp command, which she unwittingly obeyed. "There isn't a motel within a hundred miles of this place."

He left the room and Charly turned around to warm her backside. She noticed that the old man was nowhere to be seen in the spacious room that served both as living room and kitchen. She looked down with dismay at the muddy puddle she had made on the floor. Suddenly she was shivering uncontrollably and felt very close to tears. What in the world was she doing, getting herself into a predicament like this?

In a moment the grizzly-looking man reappeared with several items draped over his arm. He was speaking to her as he walked closer. His words were rebuffing, denouncing, but the tone was somehow soothing, gentle. "This was really stupid, you know—coming up here by yourself. A woman like you has no business in these mountains alone and whoever sent you is a fool."

Charly smiled secretly to herself as she imagined Lewis's face if he could hear this stranger's assessment of his judgment. And he would be appalled if he could see her right now, in a cabin alone with this ruffian and an old man. She could hear him now. "What a damn-fool thing for me to do . . . let you go off alone to that mountain!"

"Here is a towel and a change of clothes." The stranger held the towel for her and she moved closer to the warmth of the fire and the burly man.

"I . . . I couldn't help sliding in the mud," Charly answered defensively. This man certainly had a way of intimidating her and she wasn't easily bullied. Maybe it was because she was so cold and miserable.

He draped the large dry towel around her shoulders. "You've had trouble with that car all day. Does that tell you anything? Maybe you don't belong on this mountain. I don't want you interfering."

She again felt his rebuff of unfriendliness. How could he be so unpleasant when he didn't even know her . . . and she was so cold . . .

Shivering visibly, she muttered, "I'm not here by my own design, I can assure you. But I can't see that *you* belong here either." That was a matter she intended to take up at a later date. "Mr. Simms is supposed to live alone."

"Well, as you can see, he doesn't." He pulled her closer to the fire.

Charly hovered near the fire, muttering through chattering teeth, "Thanks for changing my tire today. You left too soon for me to tell you how much I appreciated it. Only now the car's mired in mud that covers the tires. Oh, what a mess." She watched the reddish licking flames and tried to absorb their warmth. But her body was too wet, too chilled. All she could do was shake.

His voice was almost consoling. "We'll check out the car tomorrow. But right now you must get these wet clothes off or you'll never get warm." As he spoke, he began unbuttoning her blouse.

Mentally Charly agreed with what the man was saying, although she didn't answer. She could only nod, for she was too chilled to respond to anything but physical warmth. His voice soothed her and she stood still until his hands brushed her cleavage.

Shrinking away from his touch, she tried to cover herself, but the buttons were already undone, and the blouse was hanging loosely open down her front. Before she could grasp the moment, his rough, responsive hands were on her shoulders, pushing on the blouse.

"W-What are you doing?" Charly gasped, knowing full well what he was doing. "Get your hands off me!"

His voice was low and calm. "I'm *only* taking these wet clothes off. You can't keep them on. You're chilled. Come on, now."

"I can take my own clothes off, thank you!" she shrilled, oblivious to the humor in her words.

But the mountain man was fully alert to her words . . . and her body. He stared at her with a bemused expression, his blue eyes penetrating her . . . undressing her further.

Abruptly, the expression changed and a dark, foreboding veil covered his face. Roughly, he draped the large towel around her shoulders again. "Do it, then," he rasped. "Get all of your wet clothes off and—for God's sake—cover up those damned nipples!"

Charly looked down at her disheveled appearance. Her thin, wet blouse and lacy bra clung to her shape, outlining her breasts and pointing out the prominent nipples. Under cover of the towel, she quickly shed her blouse, letting it drop to a soggy heap by her feet. Her wet bra was next, and she huddled into the thick towel, trying to wring some warmth from the thing. It had a fresh, clean fragrance, reminding her of fields of flowers.

31

"Here are some dry clothes," the man commanded, shoving them into her arms. "Put them on."

He walked away from her and into the kitchen, which was just an open area in the far corner of the big room.

Charly turned her back on him and, with shaky hands, donned the shirt he gave her. It was a soft blue chambray, obviously well worn. It felt deliciously warm and soothing to her cold back and arms and it, too, had the marvelous fragrance of fields and flowers. In a moment her once-gray front-pleated slacks joined the wet pile of clothes and she pulled on jeans that hugged her hips but gaped widely at her slim waist.

Once again the bearded man was by her side. She hadn't even heard him approach.

"Here, drink this," he ordered, handing her a small glass.

"What is it?" She sniffed at it curiously.

"Wine," he answered shortly. Stooping down, he began to roll a cuff on each of her pant legs. "How do these fit? They're a little long, but this will help." By the time he'd finished talking, he was standing again. "Do you need a pin for the waist or will they stay up without it?"

"They're fine, thank you," Charly murmured. She didn't want to inconvenience him any more than she had already.

"Go ahead. Drink your wine. It'll be good for you." He scooped up her wet clothes and made another trip to the kitchen. Soon he returned with a small pan. Setting it down beside her, he again issued an order. "Wash your feet here. I'll get you some warm socks."

Charly sipped the pungent wine and did as she was told. By the time he had returned with the socks, her feet were washed and snuggled into the towel. She was just realizing how icy cold they were. She finished off the wine, then stuffed her feet into the large woolly socks he offered.

She smiled with pleasure. "Oooo, those feel good. Thanks. And what kind of wine was that? It's very good."

"Blackberry."

"Blackberry? I always thought blackberry wine was very sweet."

"Not the way we make it up here."

"You make it?" she asked incredulously.

"Sure. Drink it all. It'll help warm you up. There's plenty more. Whenever you're ready to eat, supper's on. Just help yourself." He refilled the wineglass, then walked away, leaving her to sip the wine and stare into the fire, pondering her situation.

Vaguely, Charly could hear sounds of the two men eating in the small kitchen area, and wondered where Simms had disappeared to during her conversation with Noah. Finally the savory aroma of whatever they were eating reached her and she realized that she was starved. If she was waiting for another invitation to eat from the men, she soon realized that she wouldn't get it. So she rose and walked meekly across the room to them.

"Do you mind if I eat, too?"

Walter Simms didn't say a word to her. He didn't even look up at her. His attitude clearly told her that she was basically unwelcome here.

Well, she thought remorsefully, I certainly don't relish the idea of being here either, so we're even!

The bearded man motioned toward the stove. "I told you to help yourself."

"So you did. Your politeness overwhelms me. Please, don't get up. I can help myself." Charly stalked angrily over to the simmering pot and dipped some of the savory stew into her waiting bowl. No one spoke, so she sat at the huge round table with the two men and ate quietly. No one said a word for long, merciless minutes of agonizing silence. Finally, in an effort to redeem the situation, if not the evening, Charly attempted conversation.

"You know, I've met Mr. Simms, here. But, although you've changed my tire and I'm now wearing your clothes, I still don't know your name."

The man gazed at her for a moment, a devilish gleam barely detectable in his intense blue eyes. "I'm Noah Van Horn. And this . . ." He paused, giving dramatic emphasis to the sounds of rain still pelting the tin roof of the cabin. "This is Noah's ark." He laughed heartily and poured another round of blackberry wine. "How do you like it?" He motioned to the wine container.

Charly's brown eyes caught his. "Which?" she asked smartly. "The ark or the wine?"

He leaned forward, his elbows resting on the table as he grinned. "Both!"

She shrugged indifferently. "The wine's fine."

He raised his dark eyebrows. "And the ark?"

Charly was not amused by his line of dialogue. "I'm not here by choice, remember."

He leaned back in his chair and motioned dramatically with his hand. "Well, city lady. You may as well get comfortable and enjoy it, because it looks like we're here for the duration. All of us together! Forty days and forty nights it rained! And they came into the ark, two by two. We haven't figured out just where you fit into the scheme of pairs, Miss Ryan. But we'll work something out, I'm sure."

Charly cringed at his wicked grin, which was barely visible under the mass of his beard and mustache. She could feel her cheeks tingle with anger as she retorted, "You don't have to worry about me, Mr. Van Horn, because I'm leaving this barbaric place tomorrow. And you can be assured that the reports I file will not be favorable toward Mr. Simms and whatever is going on up here in the mountains!" She shoved her bowl away.

"Oh, come now, Miss Ryan. Let's not get snippy!

34

Would you like more squirrel stew?" Noah offered politely.

"Squirrel stew?" Charly choked out the words. *"Squirrel? No!"*

"Yes. It's the house specialty," he admitted with a proud smile.

He lifted the wine decanter again and Charly eagerly held her glass out to be refilled. Something had to take away the funny taste in her mouth and help soothe the sudden flip-flopping of her stomach at the thought of having eaten squirrel stew. She gulped at the wine, losing count of the number of times her glass had been refilled. But right now she really didn't care. Just the thought of what she had eaten sent chills down her spine, and she wanted to drown out the sensations.

Charly sputtered angrily, "This . . . this meal will be included in my report that goes to the Bureau of Land Management in Atlanta tomorrow." She couldn't bring herself to say what it contained, but it would certainly be written in the report.

Noah folded his arms across his chest. "I'm just curious to know how your report is going to make it to Atlanta tomorrow, when you won't even be able to plow out of here for days." His mouth curled into a mocking grin.

Charly's eyes rounded in alarm as she snapped, "I am leaving this place tomorrow! With my reports! Squirrel indeed!" She shoved her chair back with a clatter and, taking her wine, stomped over to the fire, where she plopped into a stuffed chair with her back to the men.

She burned with indignation as she could hear them laughing at her outburst. But she didn't lower her dignity to give them a glance. Charly curled her feet under her in the big chair and was surprised at its comfort. Maybe she was just so tired and frustrated from the events of the day that the cozy chair provided just the security she needed. In the background she heard faint sounds of the men moving around the kitchen. As she slowly sipped her wine, Charly actually began to relax. The fire crackled busily, and soon the sight of the licking flames and the snapping noises they made consumed all of her attention.

She thought of Lewis and what he would say when he found out about her predicament. She cringed inside as she thought about facing him again and what he would say after "I told you so!"

Why had she fought his opinions? Why did she really feel so strongly that she had to prove her superiority to him? Now she would have to admit defeat, which was worse than accepting help at the outset. Damn! What it would mean was that he was right. His judgment, at least in this particular situation, was farsighted and correct. Everyone in the department would know it. And Lewis wouldn't soon let her forget this mountain situation.

Stubbornly, she didn't care. She would handle the job— and Lewis—when the time came. Right now, she'd give anything to see his handsome face and feel the security of his arms. Do I really mean that? she thought. After the way I fought his dominance, his advances? At least he would rescue me from this mountain prison, and that's what I want right now.

Charly knew that she had wanted to prove herself to Lewis. He had been relentless in his efforts to seduce her. Maybe if she had agreed to his wishes long ago she wouldn't be in this predicament. She had always been strictly business whenever she was with him. Now, in a moment of weakness, she wondered why she had refused him. Perhaps it had to do with love, or lack of it. He had promised that he would take care of her.

Still, she had resisted his every advance, and it had put her in a very difficult position with her boss. She wanted him to guide her in her career, to be her leader, her boss, not her lover. But he had other ideas for the attractive lady who was the new deputy assistant. Tonight, however, she would welcome him with open arms, just to get away from here. Oh, Lewis . . . Lewis . . . where are you when I need you?

Charly heard music floating faintly through the darkness. A radio . . . no, was it a harmonica? Anyway, it was nice and peaceful. She sipped the last of the blackberry wine and settled back in the comforting arms of the old chair. Eventually the wine and the flames worked their magic, mesmerizing her, and Charly drifted to sleep.

Vaguely, she felt herself floating, or was she being lifted? She grasped hard shoulders and snuggled against the warmth of a broad chest. A faint whiff of the smoky, masculine scent reminded her of the fire and the lovely flames that enticed her, captivated her.

Then she was being carried away from the flames, the heat, and tucked into a cool place. Frantically, she clutched at the warmth, embracing it, pulling it to her. She had been so cold, so wet, and she didn't want to lose that delicious warmth again.

Fervent hands pushed her legs straight into the cold bed, trailing, caressing the length of her limbs, lingering on her thighs, hips, waist. Subconsciously Charly clung to his warmth. Immediately, his responsive length stretched beside hers, wrapping long arms and legs around her, warming her with his passionate body. As his lips met hers, soft hair tickled her face and she accepted his hearty affection. The sensation was so lovely, so pleasing . . .

Then, with a sharp cry, she was awake, pushing against his firm chest, trying to break the steel-hard arms locked around her. She struggled—fought—against him for a moment. Abruptly, he grabbed her shoulders with a fierce jerk.

"Calm down, you wildcat! I'm here tonight by invitation!" His voice was thick and his breath fell in raspy spurts on her face.

"You . . . you are not! Get out of my bed! Why . . . you . . . you barbarian!" Charly sputtered.

He loomed over her menacingly, his entire body leaning prominently against her. "This is *my* bed, and I'm here at your insistence."

"No you're not! I didn't—"

He was so close that she could feel his hot breath on her face. "Oh, yes you did. I have the claw marks to prove it! Don't tempt me like this again or there will be *no* stopping!"

Angrily, he abandoned the bed, leaving a cool draft where his warmth had been. And Charly was fearfully alone in the dark.

CHAPTER THREE

Muted light filtered through the tiny square window, spreading a small ray of grayish luminosity over the bed where Charly lay. She blinked, focusing on the unfamiliar room, the strange sounds around her, her preposterous situation. As she tried to pull it all together in her mind, she looked around the room at the crudely built bookshelves along one wall, full of thick, hardbound books. Somehow they seemed incongruously out of place in this backwoods cabin. Perhaps it was the strings of dried onions, peppers, and some kind of—was that *meat?*—hanging at intervals along the bookcase that created the absurd kaleidoscope. There was very little else in the room except for one small desk littered with papers, pencils, and a few more books along with the bed where Charly curled, warm and dry.

She listened intently for a moment and was startled wide awake at the steady plunking, almost rhythmic beat of rain on the roof. It was quite distinct when she concentrated on the sound. Rain! *Still* raining? It just couldn't be! Charly had to get out of this place today! And how could she if it was *still* raining? Instantly, she sat up, her mind racing. She just *had* to get down off this mountain today! She threw back the covers and glanced carelessly at the bed, which, until now, she had taken for granted. It was comfortable, dry, and warm, and—had she really crawled into this bed with *that man* last night? She shuddered

39

visibly at the thought. Yet she remembered clinging to his warmth, her actions inviting him to join her. And he had! But then he had left her alone. Hadn't he? She checked her clothes and, with some relief, found them intact. With great determination she climbed out of the big bed. She had a lot to do today, the first of which was to get her car unstuck so she could leave this loathsome place.

There were other sounds that struck her as she reached for the door. A cheery, crackling sound obliterated the rain noises and Charly curiously peered into the big room. A rich aroma reached her nostrils and she was aware of the marvelous morning smells of fresh-brewed coffee and fried ham.

"Mornin'," came the almost cheerful greeting from the kitchen, where old Walter Simms was clattering around, obviously cooking breakfast.

Apparently he had decided to speak to her today, and Charly answered agreeably, "Good morning. Is it *still* raining, Mr. Simms?"

He nodded. "Yep. We've got us a real toad strangler out there. Looks like we'll be here for a while, so why don't you just call me Walt? Noah does."

Charly looked curiously at him. His figure of speech amused her, but she disliked the thought of being stuck there long enough to understand the old man and know him on a first-name basis. She just *had* to get out of here today—and she would, too. Mention of Noah's name reminded her, with chagrin, of her encounter with him last night and their eventual seductive involvement. Yes, she *had* to get away from here. If she landed in bed with that man on her first night, what would happen if she stayed longer? Well, she certainly wouldn't hang around to find out, Charly told herself. She was determined to leave today.

"Have some coffee," Walt offered, handing her a cup of the hot black liquid.

"Thank you, Walt." She ambled over to the window and gazed outside, where everything was lost in a misty gray background. "Speaking of . . . Noah, where is he this morning?" She tried to sound casual instead of curious.

"Oh, he's out huntin'," Walt answered.

"Hunting? In the rain?" Charly wrinkled up her forehead. She couldn't imagine going out in that miserable weather.

"Sure. Best time for huntin' squirrels," Walt answered easily.

Suddenly Charly was jolted back to the awful reality of her location and her reason for being there. *Squirrels?* And he was *hunting!* That was part of the problem with this particular lifetime-lease situation and now she was thrown right into the heart of it. Lewis would be interested to learn all she had to say about this place.

"Oh, Mr. Simms . . . where is your . . ."

Walt looked up curiously at her for a moment. Then he nodded knowingly. Motioning toward the back door, he said, "Out there."

"What?"

"Out there. You can go out there. Wear my old coat and boots. They're just outside the door on the porch. Go ahead."

Charly stood dumbfounded for a long moment, her eyes traveling from Walt's face to the back porch, past the neat garden, to the little outhouse, which she could barely see through the fog and rain.

"Go on before the rain gets harder. And call me Walt."

Charly was appalled at the thought of having to use outdoor facilities! It was uncivilized—crude. This was modern times and people didn't live like this anymore! As she stood there, staring outside and stewing inwardly, Charly realized that if she was to get any relief she would have to go down that path! Furiously she jerked the door open, and with angry, shaking hands she pulled on Walt's stiff coat and boots and proceeded to slosh through the mud down the path. How in the hell could she have let herself get into a predicament like this?

Later, as Charly stood by the fire warming her chilled body, frustration mounted within her and tears threatened. She pursed her lips, trying desperately to keep from crying when the unwelcomed tears burned her large, brown eyes. Walt had refilled her coffee mug and, as she sipped it, she couldn't help thinking of it as somewhat of a peace offering. His old gray eyes seemed to know of her dismay. What a way to start the day! It just made Charly more determined to leave as soon as . . . But it was *still* raining outside.

She looked up bleakly and Walt stood before her again, handing her another offering—a plate of food.

"Here, have some breakfast."

"Thank you," she mumbled weakly.

Without hesitation, Charly took the dish and sat on the edge of the hearth, remaining close to the warmth of the fire. For some reason she was starved and the ham, biscuits, and honey smelled delicious. Walt sat quietly nearby and drank his coffee. He offered no apologies, no opinions, no suggestions for her deliverance from the mountain prison. Apparently it didn't occur to him that anyone would want to escape his abode. Between bites Charly questioned him.

"Who is that man living here with you, Mr. . . . uh, Walt?"

"Name's Noah Van Horn," he answered simply.

"I know that. I mean, who is he to you? A relative?" she probed.

"Nope. A friend."

"How long has he been here?"

"About two years, off and on."

Charly squinted at his expression. "Off and on?"

Walt was not prone to long, involved communications

42

and tended to converse in short, terse statements. "Yep. He comes and goes."

"Then he doesn't live here all the time? He uses this place as a—a lodge?" Charly figured aloud.

Walt stirred, irritated with her persistence. "Look, Noah comes here and I don't question him. He leaves, and I don't question him. He is my friend and can come to my home anytime he wants to and stay as long as he wants. And I don't ask half the questions you do!"

Charly answered him firmly. "Walt, you must know this changes the account I'll have to make. You were reported to have no one else living here, but the presence of Noah changes all that. It appears that he is using this place as a recreation domicile from which he can pillage the land. It makes the chances of your staying here in jeopardy. There isn't supposed to be anyone else living off this land and it certainly isn't to be used as a . . . hunting lodge."

Walter Simms leaned back and squinted his gray eyes angrily at her. "That so? Well, let me tell you something. I won't let any city gal with a bunch of big words come up here and tell me what to do with my land or my house!"

Charly blinked, knowing that she had struck a brick wall in trying to convince this old man that her words carried a great deal of authority. So she decided on another tactic. "Where did Noah come from? Why is he here?"

Walt studied her for a long moment, anger still visible in his eyes. Then he answered tersely, "Mournin'."

"Morning?" Once again Charly couldn't understand the old man's meaning.

"Yes. He's mournin' his wife and child."

The words hit Charly like a thunderbolt and she muttered weakly, "Oh." It didn't change the facts, her goal, her predicament. But it did change her point of view—for a moment, at least—as she imagined anew the presence of the dark-haired man who had eagerly taken her to bed.

43

Sounds of thunder interrupted her harried thoughts and she glanced toward the door, which Walt was in the process of opening. She could see Noah stamping his wet boots on the porch and realized that the ponderous noise came from him. He grinned through his beard and held up three dead squirrels by the tails for her to see.

"Ooooh," Charly gasped, and quickly turned her head away to block out the grisly sight. Then she hopped up and dashed to the door, angry words lashing out at the rough woodsman. "You . . . you jackass! How could you do such a thing as . . . as this? And don't hold them up for all to see! I'm not impressed with your cruel and savage activities! What kind of man are you, anyway?"

He looked at her for a moment, his blue eyes moving wickedly over her slight frame, which was still attired in his clothes. "I am a normal man, make no mistake about it. But don't be offended by these." He gestured toward the animals. "I'll fix them in a dish tonight that you'll love."

Charly could feel her hair rise, prickling the back of her neck. "Don't bother! I'll be gone by then! It'll be a cold day in hell before I eat . . . that!" She motioned, still unable to say the words that offended her so. "Anyway, I'm leaving today."

The man laid the offending animals aside. "Oh, really? And how do you propose to do that? It's still raining, or haven't you noticed?"

"I've noticed. But at least it's daylight and I can see to get the car free. If not, you can just take me in that truck. Or I'll walk if I have to, but I'm leaving this damned mountain today!" Charly's cheeks glowed pink in her angry tirade toward the man who viewed her with mirth in his half-hidden face.

"We'll see, Wildcat. We'll see. Now, do you want to help me clean these?"

44

"No!" Charly fairly screamed at him and wheeled back into the house.

She retreated furiously into the little room in which she had spent the night and slammed the door so she could pace the floor alone. Back and forth she walked, from the door to the desk, the desk to the door. She looked up at the small window, where occasional gusts of rain blew against the panes, reminding her that the water continued to fall and she continued to be a prisoner. Well, she wouldn't be for long. She would force that barbaric man to drive her back down the mountain. Force him? She rearranged her thinking slightly and acknowledged that she would ask him—kindly. But she was sure he would do it. After all, he probably wanted to be rid of her almost as much as she wanted to get away. Could she trust him to drive her? But she quickly put that thought away. Of course she could. He hadn't bothered her when she had told him to leave her bed. She shuddered to think of what might happen if he wanted to take full advantage of her. It was up to him, for she would be practically helpless to defend herself. She should be grateful . . . *No!* She would only be grateful if he helped her get out of this godforsaken place.

Charly could hear noises on the back porch and her imagination went wild. She had to get away from the sounds—all the sounds. So she opened the door to the room and dashed out onto the front porch. Now! All she could see—and hear—was the rain plunking on the tin roof, pelting the foggy clearing and whispering on the misty forest. She settled into an old rocking chair at the far end of the porch and rocked furiously while she stewed over her helpless predicament.

Eventually a noise at the front door gave notice that she would have company. She refused to look in the direction, but could feel the dominant presence of Noah as he took

45

a chair near her. He offered no conversation at first, but soft sounds told her that he was eating.

Finally Charly broke the strained silence. "Will you help me get my car unstuck today—please?" Her voice quivered slightly with emotion.

Noah didn't answer at first, and she glanced his way to see if he heard her. When he had her attention, he said in a low, serious voice, "I'll try to help you out. But with no letup in this rain, the chances of doing that right now aren't very good."

"Oh, I can wait. When the rain stops, can we go down and see about the car?" Charly felt almost like a child, asking for an ice cream cone.

He paused before answering. "Sure, when the rain stops we'll see about it. Meantime, why don't we try to be civilized toward one another?"

Charly looked at him sharply. "Somehow I feel like I'm the only civilized one around here! What are you suggesting, now that the squirrels are skinned?"

He ignored her stabbing remark and leaned toward her. "We can start with your telling me exactly what you're doing up here alone. What is your business?"

Charly took a breath, determined to be convincing in her explanation of the importance of her job. Although she hadn't been successful in convincing Walter, Noah was younger and probably more reasonable and aware of the power of her influential position. "I'm from the Bureau of Land Management's regional office in Atlanta. I've been sent up here to evaluate the proper usage of this land and recommend viable alternatives." There! she thought with satisfaction. That sounds official enough.

But Noah was unimpressed. He was concerned with other aspects of the job rather than its importance. "Alone? They sent a woman—like you—alone to do a job like that?"

"What do you mean, 'like me'? Of course. This is just

a routine job, Noah." Charly pulled herself up indignant-ly.

Amusement played at Noah's lips as he countered. "Is it routine for you to spend the night in your client's bed and wear his clothes?"

"No. You know this has turned into a very nonroutine experience!" Charly stormed at Noah's arrogant, laughing face. "But usually my 'clients,' as you call them, are more accommodating than you!"

His eyes penetrated her harshly as his words mocked her. "Why, I don't know how anyone could be more accommodating than Walt and I. We have fed you, and I have given you my clothes and my bed. What more do you want from us? The very land we live on?"

Charly stood up, shaking with fury at the impudence of the man. "For starters, I'd like to leave this damned place!"

"Believe me, Wildcat, I'll do everything in my power to accomplish that!" He stood, towering over her, and stalked into the house, followed by a discontented Charly.

"That reminds me," she blazed at his back, ignoring his mocking name for her. "Where are my clothes?"

Noah left the plate he had been using in the kitchen. "Out there." He nodded toward the back porch.

Charly peered in the direction of his nod and then gaped in horror. There, stretched from a short, makeshift clothesline on the back porch, were her blouse, slacks, panties, and bra!

His voice pulled her horrified eyes back to his amused face. "I washed them out for you last night, but, with all the dampness in the air, they just haven't had a chance to dry. We can hang them in front of the fireplace if you want."

Oh! She had completely forgotten about her wet, muddy clothes! And he had taken care of them himself—had washed them! How could she have been so careless? And now they dangled seductively, dancing in the wind—the thin blouse, the long legs of the slacks, that lacy bra—why did she ever choose such a frilly thing?—and her bikini panties. "I'll take them!" she gasped, lunging for the door. She couldn't imagine which was worse: to have them suspended across the windows, swinging merrily, or draped in front of the fireplace for close inspection. Of course, Noah had already done that! Damn him!

She grabbed the offending garments and hustled inside with them. She would put them in her room—well, *his* room—oh, hell—the room she was using for now. She tried to find a suitable place in the small room for the wet clothes, but finally settled on a couple of hooks from which the dried vegetables hung. As she once again paced the floor, the sight of her lacy bra draped intimately with a string of dried peppers was almost funny. Almost.

Suddenly she knew what she had to do. She yanked the damp clothes off their inappropriate driers and folded them altogether into a small, compact package and stuffed them into her purse. Emerging into the big room, she confronted Noah. "I'd like to go now. Will you take me to my car so that I can leave?" Her pink lips thinned into a determined line and her bronze eyes seemed darker than before.

Noah looked up with a surprised expression. "But it hasn't stopped raining. I told you . . ."

"I don't care what you told me," she interrupted. "I want to go now. If I have to wait for the rain to stop, I may never get away from here. At least it's daylight and I can see where I'm going."

He shook his dark head. "I don't think it's wise. That road is in poor condition and hasn't improved during the night. In fact, with all the rain it's much worse. You see, the roadbed isn't packed enough. There's no base of rocks underneath. It's just a graded path through the trees. I doubt if we can get your car out." He sat back leisurely on his haunches and Charly could see that he'd been sharpening a huge hunting knife. He made no effort to move.

There was something about his arrogant, leisurely, know-it-all attitude that infuriated Charly and she found herself raging at him. "Get up! You can take me down there in your truck! And if we can't get the car out, then you can just take me all the way back to town! After all, I'm . . ." Her voice was shrill and almost out of control.

Immediately he was beside her, grabbing her forearms with his powerful hands, shaking her slightly. He pulled her close to him and Charly found herself looking directly into his forceful mouth; past the black beard, which appeared wiry, but she knew it felt like velvet; past the white, white teeth, the occasional flip of his pink tongue as he at once assailed her and calmed her with words that tumbled in short breaths on her face.

"Hey, Wildcat, get ahold of yourself. You're not going anywhere in this rain. Didn't I tell you last night we're in for *days* of rain? Now, just calm down. You'll leave here when I *say* you can and not until."

Momentarily Charly was mesmerized by his power and the absolute authority of his words. Involuntarily she swayed toward him, seeking his strength. Then, abruptly, she was shoved away from him. She stood before him, drawn magnetically toward him, although they weren't touching. Finally she found her voice. "I . . . I want to leave. Will . . . will you take me?" She felt weak, drained, like a child again, this time not asking but begging for a treat. She hated that feeling, and at that instant she hated this ruffian called Noah.

He looked at her steadily. "No. I will not take the truck out onto this mountain road and risk getting it stuck, too. That's insane." He turned away from her and stooped to continue the job he had started.

Charly spoke above the nerve-wracking grinding of

steel on steel. "Well, I'm . . . I'm going. I'll just go by myself." She paused, waiting for his response.

There was none. He didn't even look up at her.

"Thank you for everything—the food, the clothes . . . Oh, I'll see that you get your clothes back." She looked down at her attire—the blue worn shirt, the baggy jeans, her bare feet. "I'm going now."

He still didn't give her any recognition, continuing his hateful chore.

She walked to the door alone and onto the front porch, where occasional gusts of wind blew wet spray into her face. She looked at the steps and there, on the bottom step, were her smart wedge-heeled shoes, pelted into an unhappy heap where she had left them last night in the rain. She skipped over them as she scampered purposely out into the rain. Before she had gone any further than the clearing, while the house was still in sight, Charly heard a shout. Turning, she saw Noah striding toward her through the rain. He held a coat in one hand and a shovel in the other. As he reached her, she could see he was angry—extremely angry. Charly turned away from him and felt something slap her on the back, and she was roughly pushed into the heavy, stiff raincoat that belonged to Walt. She had worn it earlier in the day for her trip down the outhouse path. She allowed herself to be dressed in the coat, but refused to look again into Noah's face until he turned her himself, buttoning the front.

Forced to look into his rain-streaked face, Charly noted with distraction the drops of water that glistened and clung to his curly beard. She had a brief, wild desire to lick those silvery drops away and bury her face in his dark beard.

But he broke the spell, railing angrily at her, flashing those white teeth. "You are the damnedest, stubbornest, most hardheaded female I've ever seen! Don't you have any sense in that thick head of yours? I told you what it was like out here! Don't you believe me? I guess you don't, or you wouldn't be out here. Well, let's go and I'll show you that this is absolutely impossible, futile, and a useless waste of time." He pushed her along with him as he strode across the mud and rocks. "This is crazy and one of the most damn-fool things I've done in a long, long time. I've never met such an obstinate female!" He continued his tirade as they sloshed along. She guessed it made him feel better to justify why he was following her. So Charly was quiet. She made no comment and allowed him to vent his anger and frustration on her while they made the arduous slow trek through the mud. At least he had come along with her, and he had brought a shovel, so he intended to try to help her. And that's all she wanted. For she knew that with a little help she could dislodge the car and leave this damnable mountain. And she wanted that fervently.

At last the white compact car was in sight—barely. It was tilted sharply to one side and appeared to be buried up to the fenders in mud and tall grass. The futile, sad sight of the vehicle made Charly want to cry. She knew—at that moment—it was absolutely, totally useless for them to try to release the car from its muddy grave. Noah was right.

She stood immobile, gaping forlornly at the sight as Noah made some attempts to free it. With the shovel, he dug around each sunken fender. Then he walked around the car, assessing the extent of the problem.

Finally he straightened and returned to her, his boots and pants legs covered with mud. "It's impossible for us to get it out alone. Even if I could dig down to the tires, we would need another vehicle to help pull it out of the hole it's in. The car slid into the drainage ditch to the side of the road and . . ."

His words spelled the dismal future to Charly and she hated to face the inevitable. With tears in her brown eyes, she said stubbornly, "Then I'll just walk out of here." Her words were punctuated by a loud crack as lightning flashed somewhere near them, followed by a ponderous thunderclap.

His voice was thunderous above the sounds of the gathering storm. "Another electrical storm is brewing. You can't walk out of here. It's too far and too dangerous."

"I'll show you! I'll go where I want to go!" Charly answered fervently and brushed past him.

She had barely taken two steps when she felt a strong force on her arms, wheeling her around.

"You are not walking out of here. I'll see that you get out safely, but not now. Not today. You'll just have to wait." His voice was a threatening rumble.

Charly jerked free of his grasp. "I won't wait! You won't tell me what to do!"

"I just did!" His arm shot out to impede her passage.

Suddenly, before she knew what she was doing, Charly was screaming at him, flailing at him, kicking his legs. The more viciously she fought him, the tighter, closer he held her. She twisted, slapped, kicked, tried every trick she ever knew from fighting with her brothers as a child. But he just held on to her, not letting go, holding her close. His restraint checked the force and damage of her lashings, but that didn't deter the vigorousness of her assault. She vented every frustration of the last twenty-four hours on the man who held her, preventing her from leaving.

Eventually the force of her energetic flinging plummeted them to the ground and they rolled together, fighting, sliding, oozing through the slimy mud. Heaving with exhaustion, Charly finally stopped fighting. She was defeated. She felt the mire under her neck and hands and in her hair as Noah sat lightly astride her, pinning her arms above her head.

"Okay, Wildcat, are you ready to go back home?" he hissed.

"Home? It's not my home—nor yours either!" Charly

spat through gritty teeth. "I hate you, Noah Van Horn. I will never forget this . . . this atrocity. You'll be sorry you ever stopped me! I'm a government employee, remember, and I'll report every bit of this . . . assault. People will be looking for me."

"Oh, shut up. I'm already sorry! I'm sorry you ever set foot on this mountain with your big brown eyes and skinny hips and big breasts! Now get up and come on. You're a miserable sight now." He pulled Charly to her feet and held tightly to her wrist as they made their way, stumbling back up the mountain through the storm, back to the cabin prison.

CHAPTER FOUR

By the time they had worked their way back to the cabin in the storm, Charly was thoroughly wet, even though she wore the old man's coat. She could feel her hair matted with the spiteful mud and she resented the fact that, in her mind, Noah had caused the mess she was in now. The storm bristled around them and Charly cringed as a streak of lightning flashed in the clearing. It hadn't occurred to her that if she continued down the mountain road she would be in the midst of this same storm—by herself.

Once again she was wet and cold and tired, and once again she was seeking shelter in the remote cabin. As they ran around to the back of the house, Charly wondered briefly if Lewis had tried to reach her, if there was a faint chance of her being rescued tonight. No, he probably wouldn't even miss her yet. She'd only been out of touch with the world for twenty-four hours, and yet she felt that she'd stepped back in time and had been away for days.

"Just leave the coat here and I'll get a pan of water for your hair. We have to wash that mud out of it. Then I'll show you the shower." Noah's tight, commanding voice interrupted her rambling thoughts and she looked up to him. But he was too busy to give her any more attention, removing his muddy boots and entering the house to emerge moments later with a small pan of water.

This time he looked at her, his blue eyes sharply cutting into her as he snapped, "Well, come on, Wildcat. Get with it. We have a job ahead getting that pile of hair clean. Drop the coat, sit down here, and lean your head back. I'll get most of the heavy mud out now, and you can shower it cleaner in a few minutes."

Charly did as she was told. The fighting spirit was gone out of her now. She had been defeated and knew she would be spending another night in the loathsome cabin. She wasn't sure when—or if—she'd be leaving her unusual prison. Oh, God—what if—but *no*, Lewis would find her . . . eventually. He would surely alert the authorities. She wouldn't have to remain here forever.

Charly felt the gentle tugging on her hair as Noah worked to clean it. She gasped as its icy chill touched her scalp. He hadn't even bothered to warm it up.

"Sorry the water's so cold. One of our inconveniences up here is lack of hot water. And I didn't take the time to warm it." Noah apologized and continued his task of washing her hair.

"*One* of the inconveniences?" Charly snapped harshly. "The biggest inconvenience is *being* here!"

"Oh, come on, Wildcat. When you get used to it, it's not so bad up here. Why don't you try to enjoy the simple pleasures? Haven't you ever had to make the best of a situation?" His voice had mellowed as the anger faded.

Apparently he had decided to make the best of it—or, Charly feared, take advantage of it. The first pan of water was tossed out and another quickly replaced it. This one was warm. Charly was lost in the pleasurable sensations of Noah's hands working with her hair, massaging her scalp, tugging, stroking the length of it. She closed her eyes briefly, daring to enjoy the hypnotic motions of his long fingers. She signed, relaxing in spite of her anger, her tenseness. Perhaps she should just make the best of it and resign herself to another night here.

"There!" His rumbling voice interrupted Charly's trance. "That's as good as I can do. You'll have to clean

55

the rest off in the shower. Come on, and I'll show you where it is."

She rose and followed him down the steps and under the eaves of the house to a small square platform of bricks. Charly looked up and saw with alarm the bare shower head.

"Not very fancy, but this is it," Noah admitted.

"This . . . this open-air contraption is the shower you expect me to use?" Charly sputtered.

"Sure. Why not? You turn it on here and soap and shampoo are here . . ." He proceeded to show her what she needed. "The one drawback is that we don't have hot water, so you'll have to make it quick."

"*No* hot water?" Charly gasped.

He shrugged. "Sorry. I'm not very much of a plumber. I did well to rig this shower with piped water. You see, it hooks in with the piped water to the kitchen directly above. Actually, a cold shower is good for you. It gets your blood flowing and is invigorating." He grinned at her while she gaped from Noah's taunting face to the shower head to the pipes above them and back to Noah's face.

"You're crazy if you think I'm going to shower here," she concluded.

"Where do you propose to do it?" he challenged, folding his arms and eyeing her with one raised eyebrow.

"I'll . . . I don't know. But I won't shower here, with no hot water and . . . no curtains!"

"Don't worry, Wildcat. I won't look. I'll get you a towel and a change of clothes." He was gone before Charly had a chance to protest.

She again examined the open-to-the-woods shower and decided that she would not strip down and expose herself to the world—whatever "world" was out there in the forest. She met Noah on the porch as he returned with the promised items. "Don't bother," she informed him. "I'm not using that thing."

He examined her skeptically for a moment, then nodded. "Suit yourself. But you really need to get your hair clean. And it wouldn't hurt the rest of you, either."

Charly's bronze eyes snapped as she propped her fists on her hips. "I suppose so! And if it weren't for you rolling me in the mud, damn you, I wouldn't look like this! You aren't Mr. Clean, you know!"

He grinned agreeably. "You're right, Wildcat. We both need a shower. Let's take one together. I'll help you get your hair clean and you can scrub my back!" His long arm draped around her shoulders and he attempted to turn her around.

But she stood firmly. "I'm not amused. I told you, I'm not showering there. And certainly not with you!"

"Well, if you're going to be so stubborn about it, I think I'll go ahead. Why don't you come down and hold my towel for me? If you promise you won't look." His rumbling laughter followed him down the steps while Charly looked away angrily. He was getting his laughs at her expense, and she was furious—furious at him for making her return to the cabin and furious with herself for getting into this predicament in the first place.

Charly folded her arms and sat stubbornly on a nearby stool on the porch. She knew she was too muddy to go into the house and wasn't sure what her next move would be. She could hear the splash of the shower beneath the back porch as it mingled with the continued, steady rainfall. It was accompaniment for faint sounds of a male voice singing about Smoky Mountain rain. It reminded her of the country tune she had heard on the radio as she headed up the mountain the first day. Was that only yesterday? She tried not to pay attention to the low masculine singing and concentrated on what to do next. Somewhere in the back of her mind she knew that she would eventually have to give in and bathe in that infuriating shower. And, of course, Noah knew she would, too, which made her even

57

more resentful toward him. He was an arrogant, despicable, always-right ruffian who happened to be one of the most virile, sensuous males she had ever known. And she hated him for being that way.

Soon the sounds of water and singing ceased and Noah emerged fresh, clean, and—nude. Charly gawked at his bare body coming up the stairs toward her and only realized when he reached the top of the steps that he had a beige towel tucked low around his waist. Her eyes followed the dark trail of hair upward from the towel, the length of his flat belly, to the hairy patch that spread across his chest. His penetrating blue eyes stood out sharply in the mass of dark hair that surrounded his body and seemed to be fully aware of Charly's provocative thoughts. She felt her face blush pink and tingly as he stopped close beside her.

His hand reached out and cupped her chin, ever so gently, tilting it upward as he murmured, "You promised you wouldn't look. Go ahead and take your shower while I dress. I left your towel and clean clothes down there on a stool, so you won't have to come up like this. But you'd better hurry before I take back my promise not to look, *too.*"

He left her dazed and embarrassed until she realized that he probably meant what he said, and, if she was going to take a shower—without him—she'd better hurry.

The first blast of icy cold water took her breath and a loud shriek involuntarily escaped her lips. She was tempted to stop the shower immediately to get away from that bitter blast, but she had already soaped her hair. She rinsed it quickly, letting the water trail from her scalp, down her back, like a thousand icy needles nipping at her. She tried to discover the invigorating pleasure Noah referred to, but the chilly tingling was almost painful to her sensitive skin. "Invigorating" indeed! She was thoroughly chilled. It was such sweet relief to cut the water off.

Forcefully, she scrubbed her body with the towel, trying desperately to rub some vitality back into her cold limbs. She grabbed the clothes Noah left for her and hugged them to her. The jeans were soft and faded, and a red plaid flannel shirt had never looked so welcome and warm. Once again she gratefully donned his clothing, basking in their comfort. Wrapping the towel around her thick, dripping hair, she trooped upstairs to seek out the warmth of the fireplace.

"Have a seat by the fire and get warmed up while I fry these squirrels for supper," Noah remarked easily from the kitchen.

Charly looked at him sharply and tried to ignore the fact that he stood barechested, and that she was alone with him. It seemed that since her arrival, Simms was spending more and more of his time in his bedroom. "Don't bother frying any of . . . that for me, because I won't eat any of it. I won't." She tried to emphasize her pronouncement. He would not persuade her to change her mind about this. Taking a cold shower when you are covered with mud is one thing, but eating . . . She shuddered involuntarily as she thought about it.

He walked toward her with two small glasses of wine, amusement playing at his lips as he pressed the glass into her hand. "Well, then, how about some wine? Or is it too domestic for you?"

Charly took the glass without letting her eyes leave his. "Thanks," she murmured, raising the glass to him. "This seems to be the only pleasant thing up here."

"Oh, it's too bad you feel that way. I'd like to change your mind. You aren't offended by my being shirtless, are you? It's not exactly cocktail attire, but then we're hardly at the Ritz." A devilish grin spread across his face, lighting those flashing blue eyes.

Charly snapped him a disgusted look. "Hardly. But I'm

59

getting accustomed to the hairy bears in these mountains."

He sat on the hearth, propping his elbows on his knees, and motioned her toward the comfortable stuffed chair. His matter-of-fact answer to her caustic remark caught her by surprise. "Well, we'll have to do something about that. You can cut my hair tomorrow. I've needed a trim for a while anyway, but just haven't had a chance to get to town for one."

Charly sat in the soft chair and curled her legs under her. She answered slowly and distinctly. "When you take me to town tomorrow, you can just get your hair cut. I'm certainly not doing it."

"Don't make idle threats, Wildcat. You seem to make it a habit of eating your words! I'll show you how it's done."

She lifted her head defiantly. "Oh, I know how it's done. I could do it, if I wanted to. I just don't choose to. I have a younger brother and trimmed his hair for years until he got to be a teenager and wouldn't let me touch it anymore."

"A younger brother, huh? Is he the one who gave you the name? Short for Charlotte?"

Charly nodded with a soft smile. "Yes. Stevie couldn't say my name—it's Charlene. Sounded like 'Charly' to him and it seemed to fit, so everyone picked it up."

"Where is Stevie now? Atlanta?"

"Steve," Charly corrected. "He's trying to make me realize that 'Stevie' doesn't fit a six-foot-three twenty-two-year-old. I'm finding my old habit hard to break. He's at home in Pennsylvania. Actually, he's at Penn State."

"You're from Pennsylvania? How long have you been in Atlanta?"

Charly nodded. "I'm from Philly, and I've been in Atlanta four months now. Before that I worked out of D.C., so I've been away from home over ten years. It's funny.

60

Both of my brothers still live within shouting distance of our home, while I've been away and on my own since I was eighteen. I guess I'm too independent to stay."

"So you're the kid in the middle, huh? That makes you independent, you know. Makes you want to prove that you can do what anyone else does."

"I thought that was the oldest child who developed the strongest traits—leadership qualities and all of that." Charly smiled and sipped her blackberry wine.

Noah shrugged and walked over to get the wine carafe to refill their dwindling glasses. "Naw. Maybe leadership. But who wants to lead? Middle kids grow up proving themselves, and when they're adults they know they can do it and spin their wheels proving it to the world."

"That's a lot of psychological introspection for a back-woodsman who spins his wheels hunting squirrels."

"Hunting gives me a lot of time for thinking. Maybe that explains why you were willing to tackle this mountain as a routine assignment. Who are you trying to impress this time? Not your parents." He halted, giving Charly an opportunity to answer.

Charly replied eagerly, not realizing that she was relaxing for the first time with Noah and enjoying a conversation with him. "No. I'm beyond that. I guess I'm trying to prove myself to Lewis—my boss. He—" Charly stopped abruptly and reversed her line of conversation. "I want to show him that I can handle anything that comes into the office—that field work is something I can do, too—not just paperwork."

Perceptively, Noah asked, "Is that all you want to prove to him?"

Charly's brown eyes met his. "Yes. That's all," she answered shortly, denying with her eyes what he seemed to know. But it was left unsaid. Charly looked away, feeling that those blue eyes of Noah stripped her to her soul and knew what was going on inside her—maybe even better than she did. Yet she had only known him less than twenty-four hours. How could he be so all-knowing? It was those eyes—those devil-blue eyes that had stripped her clothes the first time she met him. Now they delved even deeper.

"Well, I'd better get busy if we're to have supper tonight." Noah rose and pulled a T-shirt over his head before going into the kitchen.

"Don't bother with me. I won't eat what you're preparing."

"Oh, come on, Wildcat. You'll like it if you give it a chance." He persuaded with humor in his voice.

"No. I won't." Charly was adamant about that. Suddenly she remembered her still-wet clothes packaged-up in her purse. She went out onto the porch to retrieve the muddy purse and the items within. Thank goodness, at least her clothes were still relatively clean. Wrinkled, but clean. She busied herself with their care, turning her back on the darkness outside, where rain continued to pelt the wet forest. When would it ever stop?

On returning, she questioned Noah. "Do you mind if I use this . . . your room again tonight?"

He smiled rakishly at her. "Of course you may use it. We backwoods people want you to know how accommodating we are! I'll even warm the bed for you . . ."

Charly turned away from his mocking face and stalked into the little room, trying fervently to escape the sounds of his laughter. She didn't think the joke very funny at all. In fact, part of her feared that he would do just that— warm her bed and her along with it sometime during the night. Another part of her desired it. After all, he was aggravatingly appealing. And both of those reasons were why she absolutely had to leave the mountain tomorrow, she resolved as she again hung her lacy bra on the hook alongside the dried peppers. She looked at the sight and laughed. Lewis wouldn't believe all this. And there were times when Charly could hardly believe it, either.

Lewis will probably be horrified when he learns everything about this miserable little excursion of mine, she thought. He is so . . . refined and smooth, damn him. In fact, in his own slick, superior way, he had been trying to get into her bed for the four months she had been in his department. And this backwoods ruffian had managed it in one night. Of course, nothing had happened—what was she thinking? It was almost as if— *Oh, no!* She just had to get away—soon! And where? Back to Lewis? Now, after this assignment failure, she might not be able to resist his advances any more. And she felt sure it would cost Charly her job if she continued to refuse him. But she was determined not to fall into that trap of his. She knew that one of the office girls spent an occasional weekend with him. The girl had not been able to keep her mouth shut, for going to bed with the boss was enough to brag about. Charly refused to join that little group. She'd request a transfer first.

Charly took the towel off her wet hair and bent over at the waist, drying it vigorously with the towel. From that position she noticed some of the books lining the wall. There was an odd assortment of everything from architecture and art to law, as well as several books on the preparation and preservation of natural foods. She supposed they all belonged to Noah and gave a general perspective of the man and his interests. But why would he need *Black's Law Dictionary* alongside *Preparing Wild Game? Foxfire* and *The Architectural Sourcebook? Drawing in Perspective* and *You and the Law?* The collection was a strange one.

Curious, she straightened and walked over to the cluttered desk. She riffled through some of the papers, with pencil sketches of everything from a simple flower to a large woolly bear rearing on two legs. Some of them were very good; some were mediocre. She assumed that they, too, were the product of Noah. This was a strange and complicated man she had encountered. Actually, he wasn't a backwoodsman at all. Then who was he? And what was he doing in a place like this? He puzzled her, yet attracted her . . .

A knock at her door startled Charly, and she jerked her hand guiltily away from the desk. She moved away from it, feeling for all the world like a guilty child with her hand in the cookie jar. Purposefully, she began rubbing her wet hair with the towel. "Yes?"

Noah opened the door slightly, giving her an outline of his towering form. "Supper's ready. Walt's not feeling well and has gone to bed. I'm all alone. Come on and eat with me."

She glared at him, trying to discern just where those deep blue eyes were in the darkness that surrounded him. "You can go to hell alone, for all I care! I told you I'm not eating any damned squirrel, and I mean it!"

"How about a little more wine?" He raised the hidden carafe.

Charly eyed the wine for a moment, then nodded, agreeing silently and trying to ignore the marvelous aroma that entered the room when he opened the door. But no! She would never admit it was a marvelous aroma! Never! And certainly not to this ruffian who poured her wine so steadily, then turned away from her without another word.

Noah ate in silence without her. Charly combed the tangles out of her hair and stood in front of the fireplace to dry it. She wondered what it would look like without the benefits of blow dryer and electric curlers. Well, she couldn't worry about that. Who cared if she looked like a witch anyway? She certainly wasn't trying to be pretty for anyone up in these mountains. She wondered briefly about Walt's illness, but Noah didn't seem concerned about him, so she dismissed her own concern. After all, he was a very old man and was entitled to feel bad occasionally.

Charly busied herself during the evening, drying her thick hair, checking on her clothes, pacing the floor. She spent a lot of time at the latter. She was extremely hungry, but wouldn't admit it and ignored the loud grumbling in her empty stomach. She hadn't eaten since the late breakfast of ham and biscuits, but that was long since gone. She had hiked—and fought—and expended a lot of energy arguing with Noah since her last meal. But she would never admit that she was hungry, especially to that arrogant man, who persisted in crossing her. And most of the time he had gotten his way. She was still here, which is what he had predicted. Damn him! He knew it all. He knew she wouldn't be leaving anytime soon. What if she were stuck here in this remote cabin all week? What if she couldn't get away from Noah? What if . . .

Suddenly Charly resorted to her remaining emotional response—tears. She had fluctuated from anger to determination to frustration during the course of the day and the only thing left to vent her feelings was to cry. It was a sudden, unavoidable, uncontrollable sobbing that racked her body and reduced her to a huddled heap on the bed. She was grateful for the darkness that enveloped her and the lonely bed where she could be alone in her misery. Her weeping continued into the night. Charly lost track of time and wasn't sure if it had been an hour or less. She just knew that she was terribly unhappy over the turn of events and wanted to obliterate it all by washing it away—with tears and the miserable, hateful rain, which still pelted the tin roof.

Charly didn't hear the door open quietly, nor did she see the large figure that gathered her in his arms. She only knew that someone was holding her close, comforting, warming her. She sought the offered solace, clung to it, cloaked herself in his protecting, secure arms.

"There, there, Charly," he murmured softly.

It was the first time he had ever called her anything but "wildcat" or "city lady." And it was nice—so nice. Her name rumbled from his low voice and vibrated from his body directly into hers. "Charly . . . Charly . . ."

She buried her face against his hard chest with its cushion of soft hair and inhaled his clean, slightly smoky, masculine scent. He held her securely, without moving, until her sobbing ceased, and she continued to cling to his security.

No words passed between them. It wasn't necessary. Shared feelings were all that mattered. They lay together for a long time, enjoying, drawing from each other.

Finally, she moved, raising her tousled head from the muscular chest that pillowed her. The crying had left her voice hoarse and she felt abashed by her stereotypical feminine actions. "Noah, I'm sorry. I didn't mean to . . ."

Noah's hand caressed her hair, pushing back a part of it that fell across her face. "You don't have to explain, Charly. I understand. I do understand."

She smiled wanly, saying, "I don't see how you possibly could. You hardly know me . . ."

He sighed, trailing his finger along her cheek. "I know you're soft, and feminine, and resent the fact that you're stuck with the inconveniences of this place. You're just too refined to find anything redeemable in a place like this—or someone like me."

She sat up and smiled. "Now, I'm not that 'refined.' You forgot what a wildcat I am."

He laughed a low rumble. "Oh, no. I haven't forgotten that. You've spiced up my dull life remarkably since you arrived, Charly."

"I know I've caused you some trouble, but . . ."

He sat up. "You've opposed me more in the last twenty-four hours than anyone has in the last two years. Everyone has been sickeningly nice to me, agreeing with me, catering to me. It's true! I know you won't believe me, Charly, but I've enjoyed your challenges. I lead a simple life now. No one here challenges me. Sometimes I miss that."

"Well, if a challenge is all I've given you in exchange for safe harbor, clothes, food, and a dry bed, you're hardly being repaid," Charly said, laughing softly.

"Oh, Charly, you've given me much more than a challenge. You've inspired me."

"Inspired you? To what? How about being inspired to fix me a little something to eat?"

He smiled and winked. "I'd love it. Come with me."

Dutifully, Charly followed him into the big room.

CHAPTER FIVE

Charly awakened to a quiet morning, with daylight filtering softly through the small window. She lay there for a moment, wondering what seemed so unusual, so stark about the place. Obviously, she was still in the mountain cabin where Noah had held her again last night, had comforted her when she cried.

She closed her eyes and smiled to herself, recalling her warm feelings of pleasure when he embraced her and held her close. Sometimes just holding, just being close to someone could be comforting. He seemed to know that, for holding her was all he had done. He made no other advances, although she knew he wanted her. She had felt his desire, known of his wishes while they were close. And yet he hadn't used his strength to overpower her. Strange man, this Noah. Strange and . . . sensual. Oh, yes, very sensual. Oh, my God! What am I thinking? I've got to get out of here—soon! Her eyes popped open and she listened.

What was so different from the other mountain morning? What—then she knew! *No sounds of rain!* There was no water hitting the roof after more than forty-eight hours! Was it possible that the rain had stopped and—

Charly bounded excitedly out of bed and ran to the window. She searched the gray sky where, for the moment, no rain was falling. She was ecstatic and quickly dressed, then opened the door into the big room, which was empty. All was quiet—not even a fire in the blackened

68

fireplace. The back door was open and she glanced out-side.

Noah stood on the back porch with his back to her. He was shirtless and faced a mirror that he had hung on the support post. Charly moved closer, watching him with interest for a few moments. She couldn't help but admire him. Noah was a very virile, handsome man. His straight back was muscular and hips slim as he stood with long legs apart, concentrating on his task. The muscles flexed with his movements, and Charly realized—with inner alarm—that he must be shaving! That marvelous beard!

Charly gasped audibly and caught those intense, blue eyes of his smiling at her from the mirror's reflection. She wondered if he knew how long she had stood there, gawking at his body.

"Morning," he greeted her.

"Good morning." Charly joined him on the porch. "You're not shaving your beard, are you?" She tried to sound casual, but the question itself was defensive.

He turned around to face her, small silvery scissors in his hand. "No, just trimming it. Don't you think it's about time? Or do you think I should shave it off completely?"

Charly shook her head and answered a little too quickly to be casual. "Oh, no! I like it. It looks nice . . . on you, especially now that you've trimmed it. It adds some inter-est and a little mystery to your image."

He turned back to his project in the mirror. "Mystery, hmmm? I thought I let it get too shaggy. Guess I didn't realize it—or care—until you showed up."

"And now you care? Since when did you start caring about my opinion?" Charly folded her arms and leaned against the house, eyeing him boldly.

His response was slow and deliberate. "I care how you feel about the beard because I don't want you to be offend-ed by it . . . when I kiss you. Women have certain feelings about these things and I'm interested in yours."

Charly answered him with a sassy grin. "I told you, it looks nice. But it doesn't really matter what I think about the way it feels . . . because I'm not interested in touching it. And you can just forget about the kissing . . ."

Noah turned around to face her again, a slight smile pulling his lips, which were more visible after the trimming. "Oh, I find it hard to forget about the kissing. You're a very attractive—and kissable—woman, Charly, and I don't want to repel you with something as controversial as a beard. Come on. Surely you want to touch it." He moved forward and, taking her hand, placed the palm against the black velvet of his beard.

His quick movement and electric touch sent jolts of fire through her, and Charly tried to respond to his taunt calmly. Her fingers caressed, then dug into the soft, dark matt. "Now. My natural curiosity has been relieved. Are you satisfied?" Her voice was tight, and she pulled her hand away quickly.

But Noah stepped closer to her. "How about satisfying *my* natural curiosity," he answered quietly, pinning her against the wall.

Charly put both hands on his bare chest as he closed in on her. Although she pushed on him, she only had time for a quick, protesting "No—" before his lips met hers in a soft, wonderfully tender morning kiss.

When he finally spoke, his voice was low. "I'm not satisfied with that, Charly. It doesn't relieve my natural desires at all. It only whets my appetite for more."

"Noah, please . . ." she begged. She couldn't believe that here he was, kissing her, at this hour of the morning—and aspiring for more. And here she was, enjoying it.

"That's my line. Charly . . . please . . . don't stop me . . ." He moved his head toward her again and she knew it would mean another kiss.

Charly pushed again, this time aware of the soft hair on his chest between her fingers. "Noah . . . Noah, stop it.

70

Please, don't. I . . . did . . . did you notice that it stopped raining?" She sputtered inanely, trying to change the subject.

"Who wants to talk about the weather at a time like this?" His voice was husky.

"I do. I have to talk to you about . . . please, move. Move back a little, Noah. Move back so I can talk to you. It may mean I ~~can go home~~." Charly couldn't even think straight with the man so close that she could feel his breath on her face. She actually wanted to bury her face in that dark beard and feel those strong arms around her again. She had never before been aroused to such free abandon by anyone, and it scared her. What this man did to her actually frightened her.

Noah sighed heavily and took two steps back from her.

"Much better." Charly smiled, trying to appear calm and collected, when underneath it all she was a wreck. "I . . . I think I'd better take a walk. Then we can discuss my leaving."

"Take a walk?" he puzzled.

She nodded quickly and headed down the steps. "Take a walk down your damned little path to your damned little out-house. Oh—I hate this place!"

His rumbling, low laughter followed her and he promised, "I'll get us some coffee and maybe we can continue this *stimulating* conversation!"

There was something in his manner, his infuriatingly arrogant words that filled her with fury as she stomped down the path. He aroused such passions within her—rage, fear, desire—oh, God! the desire—that she felt almost out of control whenever they were together. Actually, she was out of control of her feelings, as well as her crazy situation. Usually she remained cool and in command of her emotions—even her desires. Never had she wanted a man like she wanted this one. Oh, yes, she was certainly glad to be leaving this bewitching place today.

* * *

"Here, have some coffee. Do you take it black?" He met her at the back steps, handed her the cup of steaming liquid, then sat on one of the lower steps, sipping his coffee. He had donned a shirt—blue to match his eyes.

"Yes. Thank you." And she joined him, gazing morosely out at the misty forest, where it had started to rain again. "I should have known it was short-lived. The break in the rain. How long does it rain in this damn place?"

"Hell, I'm no weatherman! I told you forty days and forty nights. After that, we'll see!"

"Oh, God! Spare me forty days in this cabin!" she exclaimed, horrified.

His voice was tinged with humor, but he didn't look around at her. "How about forty nights? They could be pleasant—exciting if you'd allow them to be." He drank deeply of the dark brew.

Charly raised her eyebrows. "If I'd allow *what?* This place isn't pleasant, it's boring."

"I'm offering to make things more exciting than last night—and much more satisfying. It wouldn't be boring, I promise." His voice was low and matter-of-fact.

"Guaranteed?" she laughed. "Actually, Noah, all I want to do is to leave here." It was a lie. She wondered if he knew it, too.

He emptied his cup. "You may as well resign yourself. You're here for a while. The rain doesn't show any signs of stopping—at least any time soon."

She gazed futilely out at the forest, knowing he was right. "I'm just so . . . frustrated at being here. Don't you find this boring?"

"I'm here by choice, and I don't find it boring. I'm not here to be entertained."

"Then what are you doing here?"

"Let's take a walk, Charly." He stood and turned to her.

72

"In the rain?"

"You didn't mind it yesterday. Anyway, it's not raining very hard. Just a light drizzle. It's a nice time to walk in the forest."

Gamely, she followed him away from the cabin, and they entered the quiet green tunnels provided by the thick growth of oaks and red maples and black gums. Charly hurried to catch up with Noah's long strides. "You didn't answer my question, Noah. Why are you here?"

"I lost my wife and child in an accident two years ago. I tried to escape from my grief and ended up here."

"Noah—" Charly halted and reached out for his arm. He stopped and looked at her, his eyes deep and dark.

"Noah, I'm sorry. I didn't mean to . . ." Charly was at a loss for words, but her expression told Noah her feelings of sympathy.

His voice was gentle, almost consoling her. "It's all right, Charly. Really, it is. My wife and two-year-old son were killed in a car wreck. I couldn't handle my grief very well."

"If it's too painful to talk about it, please don't."

Noah took her hand and helped her up a sharp ravine before answering. "Not unless it's too painful for you. It's been two years since the accident. I can handle it now."

"This is none of my business, Noah . . ." Charly felt uncomfortable, but Noah obviously had settled it all in his mind.

He continued to hold tight, leading her along rapidly. Then, as if something pulled him back toward her, he slowed and looked at her. "Listen—stop walking and listen to the wind and rain, Charly."

She obeyed and stood with him, both of them tuning in to the almost imperceptible sounds of the wind whispering through the trees somewhere above them and the rain faintly falling on the leaves. It was extremely quiet.

73

"I . . . I don't hear very much, Noah," Charly finally admitted.

"I guess that's what I was looking for when I first came up here. Quiet, and not much of anything. About a week after my family was killed, I left my business and came here. It was the only place I could escape to where nobody could find me."

Charly knew she was treading on highly emotional ground with Noah, and she was reluctant to question him further. She was just quiet and let him talk whenever he felt like it.

"I will admit I was escaping—trying to. There's really no escaping, though. And I felt guilty."

"Guilty?"

He nodded. "Guilty because it was them instead of me. You know—the typical 'why am I still alive?' syndrome everyone goes through when they lose someone they love. Well, I wallowed in it, and it took me a long time to realize that I wouldn't die, too, just because I wanted to. Oh, God, I wanted to!"

"Why did you come here to the mountains?"

"Oh, I guess I wanted to punish myself, as well as escape from civilization. This seemed to be a good place for that. No civilization, or signs of it. No electricity, hard to live, no hot water—all of that."

"How did you meet Walt? Did you know him?"

"No. He ran across me. I had been sleeping out for about a week. I was sick and a sorry sight. He nursed me with some god-awful herbal tea—I still don't know what it was—and, in spite of myself, I lived."

"And you've been here ever since?"

"Not exactly. After about a year, I pulled myself together enough to go back and settle things with my business partner. Needless to say, he was surprised to see me. But I wasn't ready to enter the world again—not permanently —so I just appear occasionally, to straighten my business out and get supplies for Walt. He doesn't know it, but I've been looking out for him for the last year. He would hate to hear me say that, so don't let it slip. He thinks he's still responsible for me. And I like it that way."

"And you're telling me you're not bored up here?" Charly countered.

"Hummm, maybe. But I'm too concerned about Walt to leave him indefinitely now."

Charly stopped dead still, pulling her hand from his grasp as she motioned excitedly. "Noah, the solution is simple. Just help me move him off this mountain. He would be paid a fair market value for his home, giving him a nice nest egg, and we would see that he is placed in a good nursing home or something. Then, with him taken care of, you'd be free, and my job here would be finished. I could go back to Atlanta."

Noah's stone-blue eyes cast viciously at her. "No!" he boomed. "Walt belongs here on this mountain! It would kill him to make him leave! Can't you see that?"

"But, Noah, he'll be closer to medical facilities and . . . people. It'll be for his own good!" Charly couldn't imagine anyone, of his own free will, choosing to live so far from civilization—except Noah, of course. That she understood completely—and was sympathetic toward his reasons. But Walt—

Noah loomed menacing near her, his lips spitefully thin. "I won't be a part of his leaving this mountain. And I'll do everything in my power to keep you from changing his home. He has lived here most of his life and—by God— he'll die here!"

"Well, he just might, we're so far from medical care," Charly flared.

"So be it! It's his own choosing! And no high-assed government official—and a woman at that—is going to come in here and tell him what to do! The man is old. He doesn't have too much longer to live. Can't you leave him in peace?"

"Is that what you think of me?" Charly spewed indignantly. "Well, let me tell you, you backwoods ruffian . . ."

As Charly began to verbally bombard him, Noah turned his back on her and strode away. He didn't even turn when she called him an arrogant bastard and a goddamn fool. He just kept going, out of sight.

It then occurred to Charly that she'd better follow him if she wanted to find her way back to the cabin. So she hurried after him, rounding a large poplar tree to see Noah's receding figure with its blue shirt and shock of dark hair. "Noah—Noah, wait!"

Miserably, angrily, she trailed him back to the cabin. Finally, she reached the porch, pausing to catch her breath. She could hear Noah inside, clanking pans in the kitchen, then a muffled exchange as he talked with Walt. He was probably telling the old man about their latest encounter and her proposal. Damn him, anyway! If Noah wasn't here, she probably would have persuaded Walt to her way of thinking by now. She was still stewing over the situation when Noah appeared on the porch.

He began peeling off his shirt. "Get those scissors over there and trim my hair," he instructed, without a glance her way.

"Just who do you think you are? You don't order me around. Are you crazy?" Charly was still furious and this last insult was all she needed to set her off again.

He glanced at her, his eyes cutting into her. Then he pulled the stool close and straddled it. "Nope. Are you through calling me names?"

Charly's brown eyes narrowed and she propped her fists on her slim hips. "Are *you*?"

He sighed patiently. "Yes, Wild . . . er, Charly. And now I'm ready to get my hair trimmed. The scissors are over there. By the way, I enjoyed the walk. You make such stimulating company."

"Well, you don't! You are rude. You've been away from civilization so long, you've forgotten how to act reasonably."

"Maybe. But there are some things I haven't forgotten."

"I'm sure there are! But what can one expect from a ruffian like you?"

"I don't know. What does one expect?"

Oh, he was maddening! Arrogantly, infuriatingly irritating! Charly seethed at him. "I expect to be treated with respect."

His reply was very blasé. "So do I. Now would you please get the scissors? Trim just a little here, not too much around the ears, and even it out in the back."

Through clenched teeth she muttered, "Now why should I cut your damn hair?"

"Because I asked you to. Come on, Charly. I have a day's work ahead of me. I'll fix your breakfast when we're through—unless, of course, you can cook on a wood stove."

Charly grabbed the scissors with an angry jerk. "No, I haven't had much experience with wood stoves lately. That was more my great-great-grandmother's job!"

Charly was so angry that she fairly shook as she ran her slender fingers through his thick, black hair for the first snip of steel. With measured purpose, Noah grasped her hand with his viselike grip. He pulled her around to face him. "Charly. Calm yourself. I don't have any desire for clipped ears or a Mohawk haircut. So just cool it."

"How do you think I'm going to react when you treat me like a—a child!" She recalled all the times this infuriating man had intimidated her, including now.

He spoke precisely, dragging out the words. "Ah, so that's my mistake? Do you want me to treat you like a woman?"

Charly's undoing was her next challenge, and she knew it the minute she uttered the words. "I don't think you know how. You've been away from a woman for a long time!"

"Not as long as you think. I haven't claimed celibacy yet." In one swift movement he stood, his arms encircling her, his lips kissing hers with such skillful fervor that Charly clung weakly to his back. Her heart beat rapidly against his own powerful pounding and she responded to his demanding lips in spite of herself. His tongue demanded entry, which she readily admitted, unable to resist, unwilling to stop him. His tongue separated her lips and probed her willing mouth, setting up an undeniable motion. She felt his teeth painfully hard against her sensitive lips, and a soft moan escaped her. In another breathless moment it was over, and Noah's fierce, demanding mouth moved above hers.

"Now, let's get on with the business of the day—unless you want to finish this now."

"Noah—" His kiss had left Charly weak-kneed. And she had never—*never*—had such sensual feelings pulsing through her.

"Come on, Charly." Noah sat back heavily on the stool. He had proved a point, and she dare not press him further.

Charly rested her nervous hands for a moment on his bare shoulder. Then, slowly, carefully, she proceeded to clip his hair. As she moved around his seated frame, she began to concentrate on her job, making sure it was straight and not too short, that both sides matched. Charly wasn't even aware of her thigh brushing Noah's leg or her soft breast caressing his shoulder.

But Noah was. He had shut his eyes in a pained expression and there was no conversation between them.

That didn't bother Charly. After all, what would they discuss? That indeed, yes, he knew how to treat a woman like a woman. Or should she admit her inability to respond to anyone like she had to this ruffian? No, these things were better left unsaid. Charly diligently concentrated on the raven hair she ran her fingers through, forcing herself not to look into the sensuous face a few inches below her working hands.

Finally, in a loud rasp, Noah said, "For God's sake, Charly—*hurry!* What do you think I am, a robot? My neck's getting stiff."

She stood back and admired his hair, evaluating her job. "There . . ."

Immediately he was on his feet groping for the broom. "Thanks, Charly. Here, sweep it up while I get breakfast." He reached for the door.

"Aren't you even going to look at it?" she asked, disappointed at his abruptness.

"Ah, yes." He acquiesced and glanced in the little mirror. "Yes, Charly. Nice job. Not too short. It's good. I'll get breakfast." And he was gone.

As Charly swept, she wondered if she was going crazy. Maybe being away from the city—the challenges of her job, the various people she constantly encountered—truly had had its effects on her. First, in a walk in the rain, this stranger had revealed his sensitivity to her. He probably had not discussed his family's tragedy with many people. But he had to her. Then he ordered her to cut his hair, kissed her into submission, and left her to clean up the mess. And yet her anger had diminished and she didn't really object to the sweeping. It was just something that had to be done. Maybe it was Noah's kiss that melted her defenses. God—he aroused her senses! If she didn't leave this place soon—

"Ready to eat?"

"Uh, yes. Just a minute." Charly snapped back to the reality of her imprisonment as the rain started up again in earnest.

As the two of them ate the hearty meal alone, Charly asked about Walter Simms.

"He's still not feeling well. I took his breakfast in to his bed."

"It's not just because I'm here, is it? I hope my presence hasn't been upsetting to him. It seems he's spent a lot of time in his bedroom since I've been here."

Noah shook his head. "He has a bad heart. This happens occasionally. He just feels weak, with no energy. Anyway, I assured him that I'll handle you, and that no government agency will run him off."

The assurance of his voice jolted Charly. He seemed so positive of his ability to prevent her from accomplishing her job. They finished the meal in silence with Charly pondering his statement about "handling" her. Was that his goal? To "handle" her? Or just to protect his friend Walt? She suspected the two meshed into one effort.

They spent the day at various physical labors around the cabin. In spite of the rain, Noah chopped wood. Out of sheer boredom, Charly helped him stack it, donning the funny old straw hat Noah handed her. She even hauled in a load of wood for the fireplace, while he carried some to the kitchen's wood stove.

Noah led her to the cellar, a dank, earthen storage area dug into the side of the mountain. They chose some smoked meat for the night meal, which Noah called "supper," and Charly teasingly corrected him with "dinner."

The garden required some weeding, and Charly bent in the misty rain to help Noah. They loaded themselves with red-ripe tomatoes, fresh, leafy lettuce, and long, green cucumbers for a marvelously fresh salad for "supper."

By evening, Charly slumped into a stuffed chair, her aching body bordering on exhaustion. It had been one of those days where the physical activity had kept her busy, and that in itself kept her happy. There was something gratifying about the hard work done with her hands, and it hadn't given her time to worry about getting off the mountain. She stared into the fireplace where Noah worked patiently to kindle a flame. Soon his efforts paid off and yellowish flames commenced to flicker, growing in size and intensity as they engulfed the carefully stacked logs. It was a peaceful sight, and Charly stared magnetically at the flames and the man who coaxed them.

Noah turned around and casually placed his hand on her knee. "I'm going to take a shower before dark. How about you?" It was a casual 'will you have a cup of coffee, too?' kind of question.

Charly hesitated. She knew that after the hard working day she'd put in she certainly needed a bath. But she couldn't avert the natural protest. "Oh, Noah, that water's so cold . . ."

He smiled at her and she felt the flame's glow spread over her. "Tell you what. I'll give you a pan of warm water from the kettle that's been heating on the stove. You can take a 'bird bath' in your room. How's that sound? Warm enough for you?"

"*Bird* bath?" Charly laughed.

"That's another one of Walt's expressions. Frankly, none of it sounds nearly as much fun as 'skinny dipping'!"

She smiled at him, her bronze eyes dancing with yellow highlights in the firelight. "The 'bird bath' sounds just fine."

"We'll delay the 'skinny dipping' to another day," he warned as he braced himself on her knee and climbed slowly to his feet. "Ahhh, I'm not getting any younger after a day like this."

Charly was delighted that he evidenced the same exhaustion that she felt. It made her feel better to know that she could compete with this mountain man in his everyday life and feel no worse than he. She wondered briefly if he could compete in hers. But it really didn't matter.

By the time Charly emerged clean, if not entirely re-

81

freshed, from her little bath, Noah was returning from his shower. His hair was wet and he dripped steadily across the room. His attire consisted, once again, of a small towel strategically wrapped below his waist.

"Noah—" Charly gasped at the sight of his bare body.

"I know—I'm dripping water everywhere. Grab that towel over there and dry my back, will you?" He turned around and presented his wet, brawny back to her, the corded muscles prominent and glistening with moisture.

Charly fumbled with the towel, trying to be casual about her task. She dropped the towel, grabbed it up quickly, rubbed his back, trying to be only concerned with the water that dripped to the floor.

Finally, he turned around to face her, a devilish glow in his blue eyes. "That's fine. Thanks. Now, if you'll let go of the towel, I'll use it to dry my hair."

Charly smiled sheepishly. "Oh. Oh, yes. Sure." She released her firm grip on the towel and watched him disappear into the room she used.

"You don't mind if I use my room to change, do you?" he called.

"No, not at all," Charly hastily affirmed.

Dinner was quiet. Noah prepared a dish for Walt in his room, leaving Charly and him to eat alone again. They cleaned up the dishes together, and as they finished Noah offered, "How about after-dinner wine on the patio?"

"The patio?" laughed Charly. "Sounds magnificent!"

"Of course, in simple mountain terms that's the back porch." He chuckled.

Charly went ahead, inhaling the cool, clean mountain air. She could hear the rain falling lightly on the already-saturated earth, but the blackness made it impossible to see the forest that surrounded them. She felt lost—lost in a hideaway filled with soft, pattering sounds and slow calmness that allowed her mind to roam with no interruptions. Maybe this was just what she needed. A break, a total escape from her hectic life was rejuvenating. Noah joined her with the wine, and his very presence reminded her that she was not alone in her hideaway—nor did she want to be.

Charly took the offered glass, touching his fingers casually in the exchange. "Thank you. As much as I hate to admit it, Noah, it's very pleasant here. Even the sound of the rain is relaxing. Two days ago I hated it." She laughed and sipped from her glass. "I could become addicted to your blackberry wine, you know. This is getting to be an every night's occurrence."

"It's not Chablis Premier Cru, but it'll do, I suppose. I could easily get accustomed to a habit like this, Charly." He stood close to her, their sides touching. "You're right, you know. I have been here a long time. I have almost forgotten how nice it is to have a woman around all the time. I've enjoyed having you here, Charly."

She turned slightly, not quite able to make out his features in the dark. "Noah, you know I've been an aggravation from the beginning." She laughed nervously, trying to lighten the conversation, for she could feel the sexual tension between them.

"But I've enjoyed this . . . ." His voice trailed away as he cupped her chin with one hand and kissed her lips. Charly stood motionless as his beard brushed her face and his lips caressed hers gently. It was not the fervent, intense kiss of the morning, but a languid, tender touch that kept her desire smoldering while her senses begged for more. His hand trailed her neck, leaving a hot stream of fiery passion, stroking the cleavage between her full breasts until a small gasp of pleasure escaped her lips. The kiss intensified as his hand encircled one breast, his thumb massaging the tip to ripened perfection.

Charly strained against his hand, wanting him to stop,

yet desiring him to continue. She moaned softly and tried to move away, but a gentle tugging on her nipple forced her to stay. "Oh . . . oh, Noah . . . please . . ." she murmured, trying to talk under the force of his lips.

He moved to kiss her cheeks, her eyelids, her forehead. His hand slid from her breast to around her waist, pulling her closer to his full length, so that she could feel his rising passion. It gave her a chance to speak, but her words came out in a hoarse whisper. "Noah, please—don't. I—we—we mustn't. This is too soon."

He held her close, his lips resting against her temple. "Charly . . . Charly, don't deny what's happened between us. It's too good, and it's not too soon. It's been too long in coming for me. I want you . . . I need you . . ."

"No! Please. You'll spill my wine. Let's go inside." The earnestness of his voice scared her and she knew that if she stayed much longer, if he touched her again, she would give in to his desire—and her own burning passion. She started to move toward the door, but Noah stopped her and pulled her into his arms. This time the power, the appeal, the desirability of the man overpowered Charly's rational protests and she clung to him, returning his ardent kiss.

In a flash, she was swept up in his arms and, as he groped for the door, he murmured, "Don't spill the wine, Charly."

Instinctively, she held the glass upright behind his back, where her hands clung for support. As he lay her on the bed, she gasped, "Oh, Noah, the wine—the wine!"

He halted and moved his lips away from hers, half-expecting to feel the cool liquid splashing down his back. But she brought the glass around him with a satisfactory smile. "And not a drop spilled." She laughed triumphantly, sitting up to drink the remaining drops.

"My, my, what a marvelous sense of balance you have,

Little Wildcat," he teased, nuzzling her earlobe.

"Just natural reflexes to save good wine, Mr. Van Horn." She smiled.

"Speaking of natural reflexes . . ." His lips claimed hers, drinking hungrily of her sweetness, and the empty glass fell abandoned on the bed.

As his lips moved against hers, she allowed them to part for his tongue's penetration and exploration of her mouth. Charly became enraptured, caught up in her own longing for this man whose beard tickled her face and whose obvious desire responded to her own. She wasn't aware that his hand easily manipulated the buttons of her shirt—*his* shirt—until she felt the gentle tugging on her taut nipples as his fingers sought first one, then the other rosy tip.

Gasping with pleasure, Charly allowed his kisses to deepen, gave more room for his hand to roam, responded like she never had to any man's touch. She closed her eyes and reveled in the splendid pleasures Noah created as he brushed her eyelids with his lips, her cheeks, her earlobes, her neck—her breasts and their hard, rosy tips. She lay back flat against the bed, giving him the invitation she knew he wanted as his hand trailed lightly over her body, pausing only a moment to unzip her jeans—*his* jeans.

As his hand probed even further, he shifted to stretch to her length, one leg draped over hers. His exploring fingers discovered the extent of Charly's responses, introduced her to even greater heights of ecstasy.

"Noah . . . oh, Noah . . ." she murmured as his lips set her on fire. She arched her back to increase her pleasure but realized that his hands had stopped probing, strategically eliciting her sensuous desires to the peak he sought. Then she knew why. He lay over her, prying at her legs with his knee, and she felt him against her stomach. She knew—too late—what she had done, what she had led him to. He had warned her that there would be no stopping.

"I want you, Charly—need you . . ." he rasped, close to her face.

"Yes . . . oh, yes, Noah." And she knew that she didn't want him to stop.

CHAPTER SIX

Charly's peaceful sleep was invaded by the feathery-soft caress of a butterfly on her eyelids, inviting her to awaken to greater pleasures. The butterfly refused to go away. It continued to provoke and tickle her until her brown eyes popped open to see that the annoyance wasn't from an insect, but the light touch of a man's lips. The sleepy-eyed face of Noah was only inches from hers, and he kissed her nose and murmured, "Good morning, Wildcat. Have some coffee?"

He moved back, and Charly blinked and smiled at him. "Morning. Do you always wake your houseguests this way?"

He grinned slightly, and she could see a faint glimpse of white teeth beneath the beard. "Sorry. I lost control. Your eyelids looked so alluring, just laying there, tempting me. Anyway, I figured I shouldn't have to face the morning alone while you sleep peacefully through it all."

She paused and narrowed her eyes. "Do I hear rain—still?"

"Yep. Beautiful morning. At least, in here it's nice."

"Is that my coffee you're holding?" Charly shifted up on the pillows and reached for the steamy cup. Modestly, she tucked the sheet under her arms, hiding what he had already seen—touched. She lowered her eyes and sipped, murmuring, "Thank you. It's very good."

Noah's hand caressed her cheek, and she looked up into

his intense blue eyes. Suddenly she was filled with embarrassed constraint with this man she barely knew. She remembered the intensity of their lovemaking the previous night and knew she certainly hadn't shown any constraint then. She could see that he was fully dressed, and she wondered when he had left the bed. Last night or not until this morning? She really didn't know.

Her eyes must have told him what she was thinking, for his voice was low and gentle. "Don't be ashamed of what happened last night, Charly. It was a very honest and natural consequence. After all, I'm just a man. . . . It was very beautiful. *You* are very beautiful, Charly."

She bit her lip and looked away, catching sight of the incongruity of the books and dried peppers. *Just* a man? *Hardly!* "But I don't know you. I . . . I can't believe I let myself . . ."

His hand stretched around her jawline and turned her face back to him. His thumb gently followed the shape of her lips. "But that doesn't matter, Charly. The important things are the feelings between us right now. And those are good, aren't they?"

She looked at him quietly for a moment. Unmistakable magnetism definitely attracted her to him. She smiled broadly. "The best, Noah. The best!"

Immediately, his lips met hers in a fierce encounter that left her gasping for breath. "Oh, God, it was good. You are the best, little Wildcat!" he murmured against her face.

"Noah, the coffee! I . . . we're going to spill the coffee!"

He kissed her nose and eyelids again. "Why, you managed to handle the wine last night and didn't spill a drop! You should be able to juggle a simple mug of coffee!"

One hand weakly pushed against his chest, slipping between the shirt buttons to the dark mat of hair that cushioned it. "I don't think I have the same sense of balance this early in the morning," she said, laughing.

He sat up and clasped his hand over hers, guiding it

further inside his shirt and holding it firmly against the hardness of his chest. She felt the taut muscles and the hard nipple surrounded by velvety hairs and enjoyed the magnetic warmth of his body. She ran her hand down his rib cage to the unnatural barrier of his belt, then back up again where the steady pounding of his heart filled her palm. It was a nice feeling to caress him freely, to know he enjoyed her touch as much as she did.

"You'd better finish that coffee quickly or we'll be making love with coffee dripping from our bodies," he warned hoarsely as he set his cup on the floor.

Charly giggled. "Sounds like fun," she managed, and took one big gulp before he relieved her of the responsibility of the thing and lowered his body to hers. "Noah . . . it's . . . it's too early . . ." She squeezed the words between his kisses, and then he left her lips to make a hot trail to each uncovered breast, then returned to her protesting lips again.

"Never—never too early. It's still raining, and there's nothing else to do." His raspy voice was teasing, as was his tongue.

"Oh—oh, Noah. . . . What do you mean, 'nothing else to do'?" She tried to be insulted, but his never-ceasing kisses left her weak and willing to please and be pleased.

He undressed and came to her quickly, urgently. This time there was no hesitancy or reserve as Charly opened her arms to him. The rain beat steadily on the tin roof of the little cabin, obliterating the world from the lovers, who escaped to their hideaway only to discover everything important in each other. Their passion ascended to the zenith of their emotions, leaving them clinging to each other for the affection and acceptance they shared. It was what they both wanted—needed—and they drew from each other. Somehow it seemed exactly right, too.

Afterward, Charly dozed in his arms, her head pillowed on his chest. When she awakened, she could still hear the soft sounds of rain on the roof. It was almost like a sweet song now, serenading their lovemaking. Only a few days ago she had hated that sound. But now it was pleasant and romantic. Many changes had taken place in the last few days.

Charly looked up at Noah's still-sleeping face. He encompassed the biggest change that had come over her. Someone who had frightened, angered, and fought with her had turned out to be appealing and engaging and—sensual. Unable to resist the touch, she traced the straight line of his nose and down to where his lips parted slightly as he slept. What an interesting man you are, Noah Van Horn, she thought. And what a crazy thing I've done! I must be losing my mind—but I love it!

Unexpectedly, his mouth opened further, and his teeth nipped her finger lightly.

"Ouch!" Charly jerked back in surprise. "I thought you were still asleep. Hey! You tried to bite my finger!" She grabbed a handful of his velvety, curly beard.

He smiled, his eyes still closed as he nuzzled her earlobe. "I don't bite—just nibble around a little."

"Speaking of nibbling, I'm hungry. What does a girl have to do to get breakfast around here?"

"Oh, I guess you qualify by just doing . . . this. I think I'll finish what I started earlier this morning . . ." He started to move.

Quickly, Charly sat up in bed. "Now just a minute!"

He laughed, a deep, rumbling laugh. "Calm down, Wildcat. When I brought you coffee, I intended to prepare your breakfast and bring it to your bedroom suite. But I got sidetracked by a bewitching beauty with thick chestnut hair and big brown eyes. She's a real wildcat, too, with claws and sharp teeth!"

"Oh, yeah? Then keep her out of this bedroom! This is my domain! Where's my breakfast?" she demanded, laughing delightedly.

He bent to pick up his jeans. "At your service, ma'am. How about another cup of coffee while you wait?"

"Sounds fine," Charly agreed, and leaned back leisurely on the pile of pillows, pulling up the sheet to cover her breasts. "Just bring it into my luxurious bedroom suite, sir!" She laughed at the thought of calling the humble little room a "suite."

She looked very happy and alluring against the white sheets with her dark hair spread over the pillow. Noah gave her one last longing look, then disappeared to do her bidding.

They spent the morning leisurely, eating, laughing, talking. Charly helped Noah clean the antiquated kitchen. Looking in dismay at the old wood stove, Charly said, "I don't know how in the world you cook a thing on this. It looks like something that belongs in a museum."

"It probably does. I had to learn how to fire it up and gauge cooking times differently—slower."

"Well, if you'll fire it up, I'll start some vegetable soup. This seems like a good day for soup—and I don't have a taste for squirrel! Of course, I'll need some vegetables from the garden, Noah." Charly felt very domestic today for some reason and began to busily prepare the soup. "Anyway, it'll be good for Walt," she deducted, thinking of the old man, who still refused to get up. She wondered how much was actual illness and how much was stubborn insolence. Humming merrily, she covered the huge pot and left it simmering, while she and Noah sat on the back steps, watching the silvery rain. It was a pleasant, comfortable day. And Charly didn't mind the rain at all.

Finally, Noah offered, "I'll take Walt his lunch. Looks like he isn't going to make an appearance again today."

Charly laid her hand on his sinewy arm. "Let me, Noah. I made the soup for him, so I'd rather take it in to him. I have a feeling that part of his ailment is my being here. This will give me a chance to talk to him."

Noah looked at her honestly. "I know he's not too happy with your being here. And, frankly, he probably doesn't want to talk to you, Charly, so don't be offended if he's short. You don't exactly represent his ally, you know."

"But I'm not his enemy!" Charly protested.

Noah shrugged and let the matter drop. "Walt really does have a heart problem and is sometimes in bed for days at a time. When he says he doesn't feel well, I respect that. The doctor says there isn't much he can do for it except rest and take his medicine. And I've seen to that. He's just a stubborn old man."

"I don't care. I want to see him. Please." Her voice was tender, yet serious. "After all, Noah, I am using his home."

Noah hooted tauntingly. "I can't believe you, of all people, said that! Ms. government official, friend of the mountaineer, prepares vegetable soup for last supper! Sure, Charly, go ahead! Walt will never suspect a thing!"

"Damn you!" she shrieked, lashing out at the large man, who easily pinned her arms to her sides and kissed her lips.

"Can't you take a little teasing?" he rumbled close to her.

"Not . . . not about this . . . about my job and . . ." she sputtered.

"To hell with your job!"

"Too bad I can't say that! My job happens to be the way I live!" She jerked free and gave him a nasty look before going inside. She could hear his low-rolling laughter as she prepared a tray for Walt. Damn his insolence anyway!

Charly concentrated on making the lunch offering for Walt attractive and appetizing. She even added a small wild violet and smiled approvingly at the feminine touch. Apprehensively, Charly walked into the semidark space that Walter Simms occupied. The room was larger than the one she and Noah had shared, but not as interesting. It included a very old dresser and chest of drawers, a wooden rocker, and a lamp with an old yellowed shade. One time, many years ago, the furniture and lamp must have been new, but now they, like Walter, were withered with age.

"Mr. Simms—er, Walt, are you hungry? I've made some great vegetable soup. Everything in it came from your garden." Charly's voice cheerfully punctuated the heavy silence in the room.

Walt made no move to take the tray, so she set it on the table beside the bed. His sharp blue eyes followed her and she felt their gaze raking her back. Turning to him, she said agreeably, "Can I prop your pillows up for you? You'll need to sit up if you're going to eat."

"I can sit up by myself," he answered shortly, and began to peel back the covers. Charly was amused to notice that the old man was fully dressed. She didn't comment, but took his elbow and assisted him to the chair, where he plopped, obviously ready to receive the tray.

He eyed the soup and asked, in his short, terse way, "Say this is vegetable soup?"

"Yes." Charly nodded.

"Hmmm, haven't had vegetable soup in a long time. Bessie used to make it once a week—straight from the garden in the summer, like you did."

"Bessie?" Charly sat on the edge of the bed, relieved that she had penetrated the wall between them, even if only a crack.

"My wife," he answered between bites, as if she should recall his wife, deceased for over ten years now.

Charly vaguely remembered reading in a report somewhere that at one time Walt had had a wife. She listened as he told about Bessie and their simple, gentle mountain life. She could tell how important the life was to him— even the remembering. He talked throughout the meal.

93

And Charly communicated, but not too much, and asked the right questions at the pauses. It was the most Walt had conversed in days—even with Noah.

As she took the empty tray from him, he gazed at her for a long moment. Then, tersely, he said, "Thanks. That was pretty good . . . for a city girl." He turned and hobbled toward the bed and Charly left, not knowing if she had succeeded or not.

She set the tray in the sink and sought Noah, who was still on the back porch. She needed some kind of reassurance, but it was doubtful she would get it from him.

He looked up and grinned devilishly at her. "Undoubtedly, Walt decided to talk. For a while I was worried about you. Thought he had you cornered! You never know about these mountain men!"

"Oh, you!" She tried to tweak his ear, then slipped her arm through his as she sat near him. She snuggled against his shoulder, enjoying the fresh, woodsy fragrance of him. He made her feel good even when he teased.

"Actually, he had a lot to say—mostly about Bessie and their life together."

"Well, you must have said just the right things to bring him out like that, Charly. He can be an ornery old cuss sometimes, and nothing—or no one—can open him up."

Charly shook her head and part of her hair fell on Noah's shoulder. "I don't think it was anything I said. It was something I did. The vegetable soup reminded him of the kind Bessie prepared for him frequently. I think that brought him around. He seemed surprised that a 'city girl,' to use his phrase, could do such a thing as cook."

"So am I. Let's go in and try it. I want to see what kind of potential you have. I know what a great lover you are—but a cook, too? I may just kidnap you forever!" They rose and he swatted her playfully on the rear.

Charly smiled, but ducked her head in embarrassment at his compliments about her loving. It was too soon, and

Charly was still trying to adjust to this new relationship with Noah. Actually, her own behavior amazed her. She had never let her emotions run rampant like this. But then she had never felt like this before either.

Soberly, she admitted, "I'll bet my office in Atlanta thinks I've been kidnapped. They haven't heard from me in days. But then . . ." She paused, thinking. "Lewis has been out of town, too, so maybe no one else will worry about me."

"Who is Lewis?"

"My boss."

"And he's the only one who would worry about you?" There was an edge of concern in his voice and another question in his words.

"Well, I usually keep in touch with Lewis. So, for a few days, he's the only one who would realize that I haven't reported in or that I'm unreachable."

He pressed. "Is your boss the only one who would care?"

Charly took a deep breath and nodded slowly. "Lewis is the only one who will care. However, he will care very much that I'm staying in a cabin with two men!" She laughed lightly, but both of them realized that there were others who would one day invade their lovely hideaway world.

"Does that bother you?"

She reached up and caressed his cheek and the dark beard. "Not any more. I could stay here forever! I don't care if it never stops raining!"

His hand covered hers possessively and he moved it to his lips, kissing her palm fervently. In a moment they were in each other's arms, kissing, caressing, clinging. Forgotten were Walter Simms, their waiting lunch, the world outside. They were aware solely of each other and the passion of fire ignited by only a touch.

The days lengthened and Charly wasn't aware, nor did

she care, if the rain still fell. She was happy and busy and had found a kind of freedom that she had never known in a strange and different mountain world. And she had discovered an unmatched relationship with a man she loved. Or did she? Was it possible to love someone this soon? This intensely? Was it love—or lust? Oh—she didn't want to think about that. All Charly knew was that she was gloriously happy with Noah.

They were free and open and loving, and there was no interference from the outside world. There were no time schedules, no meetings or parties, no people except Walt.

The old man kept very much to himself. It was as if he knew intuitively, through his vast years of life experiences, that the two were in love. Sometimes he prepared dinner, then left them alone while he took a walk. Other times he serenaded them at night with the plaintive sounds of his harmonica. Who would say it was romantic? And yet to Charly the music, mingled with the quiet sounds of the mountain nights, was as romantic as Nancy Wilson's "Midnight Sun." And now she knew the meaning of the lyrics that spoke of a brilliant flash of the midnight sun as her love for Noah reached new heights every day . . . and night.

"You've been here for a week, Charly. I can't believe so much has happened in so short a time." There was wonder in his voice as they walked through the quiet woods. The constant rush of water from the mountain stream they followed was the only sound for a few minutes.

"It has been busy, hasn't it?" Charly agreed. Busy falling in love, she thought.

"Now that the rain has stopped, we should check on your car."

"Tomorrow." She answered firmly, taking his hand as they walked along.

"That's what you said yesterday. Charly, you've got to—"

"No, I don't!" she interrupted, putting her fingers on his lips. "Not today! Tomorrow, or in a few days, I'll worry about the car and . . . everything. But not now. I just don't want to! Now, are you going to show me how to catch rainbow trout or not?"

"Well, I don't know. After that loud outburst, they probably have hidden in the deepest, darkest hole they can find," he admonished her.

Charly's hand flew to her mouth apologetically. "Oops, sorry. Do you think I scared them all away? Darn! There goes our fun!"

"There goes our supper!" Noah pointed with the long fishing rod in his hand. "We'll go on upstream a bit. Maybe they couldn't hear you this far away. But remember—quiet. They can hear you."

Charly nodded, trying to be serious, but a devilish gleam lit her brown eyes. "Okay. Those little fish are clever fellows, aren't they? Just don't mention . . ."

"Leaving," Noah finished, catching her eyes knowingly.

She looked deep into those blue eyes she rapidly had grown to love and nodded. "Yes, leaving."

The conversation failed to put a serious damper on their usually jolly mood. It just pointed up—briefly—Charly's aversion to leaving or even talking of it. They climbed through thick green underbrush and over huge gray rocks to reach the small river's bank, where Charly watched solemnly as Noah cast his lure skillfully across the dark rushing waters. He pointed to a specific spot where the water ran deep and murmured in hushed tones that it was a "good hole" and likely spot for a trout. She watched spellbound as he patiently and expertly flicked the silvery lure to the exact spot time after time, reeling it slowly to skim the water's surface, then casting again to repeat the action.

Abruptly, the repetitious, monotonous action of casting

and reeling was broken as a splash shattered the water's surface and the rod bent with the weight of an obvious catch! Slowly, patiently, Noah reeled and worked with the fighting fish. Charly wanted him to raise it high out of the water so they could view it triumphantly, but he humored it, finally wading out into the icy stream to meet it halfway and dip it quickly into the net. Only then was there a triumphant smile on Noah's face as he showed her the fish with its beautiful rainbow-colored stripes that glistened in the afternoon sun.

Charly gazed wide-eyed into the net. She was like a child and everything in Noah's mountain world was a wonder. "Oooh, Noah, it's beautiful! I . . . I don't think I can eat it!"

Noah rolled his eyes. "Oh, no! Don't tell me that— Charly, that's ridiculous! This is the sweetest, best-tasting fish you've ever had—especially these mountain trout. They're delicious! Surely you've eaten fish before!"

"Yes," she countered. "But not the ones I've looked in the eye!"

"Oh, my God, Charly! What a sentimental fool!"

She folded her arms defensively. "I can't help it. I just . . ."

"I suppose if you spent much time up here you'd turn into a complete vegetarian! And then, if the carrots waved at you in the breeze, you wouldn't eat them either!"

She narrowed her eyes at him. "I suppose so!"

He shook his head and proceeded to unhook the fish and drop it into a bed of damp leaves in the creel that hung from his shoulder.

She watched him silently, then decided she would be a good sport about it and prove her willingness to adapt to his life-style. "Let me try to catch one. Teach me to fish, Noah."

He raised his eyebrows and gazed at her for a minute,

then nodded. "If you catch one, you have to eat it. Rules of the game."

She eyed him skeptically for a moment, then determinedly agreed. "Sure." Her facade was much more assured than she felt inside.

Fortunately, with the first cast of the rod, Charly was saved from her promise to the "rules of the game." The lure, hook, and thirty feet of line were hopelessly tangled into the branches of the oak tree, which spread its limbs majestically over Charly's head and half the small river. Noah spent forty impatient minutes trying to untangle it. Finally, he cut the line, leaving a portion of the mess in the tree for posterity.

"Noah, I'm sorry. I don't know how that happened! It just looked so easy to see you flip that little thing over your shoulder right to the exact spot where you were aiming." Her brown eyes were innocently rounded.

"It takes years of practice to cast the way I do, Charly. I tried to tell you—"

"You aren't mad at me, are you?"

He looked disgustedly at her for a moment, then his face broke into a smile. "No, Charly. I'm not mad at you." What could he say when she looked at him that way? Those eyes . . .

She kissed him quickly. "Good! I think I'll watch you awhile longer. I'll learn to cast another time."

"Good idea," Noah agreed tersely as he tied on a new float, weight, and lure.

Charly lounged comfortably on a huge gray rock, observing quietly as Noah repeated the casting procedure until he had netted three more large trout in the next hour and a half. It was a slow process, requiring considerable patience. Perhaps it wasn't the thing for Charly after all.

Finally, Noah turned to her, where she dozed on the sun-warmed rock. "Come on. Let's go home, Wildcat."

There was something exciting and secure and loving about his statement, and indeed, Charly felt as though being with Noah—even on this alien mountain—was "home." Immediately, she curled an arm around his waist, and arm in arm they walked through the woods toward home.

CHAPTER SEVEN

The days melded into one glorious, loving experience for Charly. Some of her time was spent in quiet reflection, alone. And Charly enjoyed that. It was like an unexpected vacation for her and a welcome respite from the dailiness of her job.

She also spent many hours with Noah, and that time was almost like a honeymoon for Charly. She grew to know him and love him, as they shared their lives with one another. He had eased his way into her heart.

During one of their pastoral walks through the forest, Noah opened a small crevice of his past. It was just enough for Charly to realize that the way to Noah's heart would not be easy. She had to climb a mountain first.

Charly's laughter echoed against the trees. "I guess I was a tomboy. With two brothers, what else could you expect? They even let me play sandlot baseball with them, but insisted that I play right field. One time, there weren't enough players for all the fielding positions to be filled. I begged for them to let me play first base. They finally agreed, and I made four outs in the game! After that I played first base every time!"

"Were you Phillies fans?"

"Oh, my God, yes! Our big—and only—family event was to go to a Phillies game. It wasn't often, but as we kids got older we worked odd jobs to pay our own way. I think it bothered our dad, but we were such a gregarious bunch, he couldn't help but go along with us. We'd pitch in and buy him a hot dog and couple of beers, and he'd be in heaven!" Charly smiled as she recalled the fun they had had together.

"What about your mother? Did she go along?" Something in his voice said he couldn't imagine such a thing.

"Oh, sure! She loved it, too. Or maybe she just went along to be with us. I'll have to ask her about that someday. Anyway, she seemed to have fun. She worked, too. She was a teacher, so she didn't make much. But it helped keep us in jeans and tennis shoes. I dressed like my brothers. Thought everybody did until I reached junior high."

"Are you still close to your family?"

Charly nodded. "As close as I can be when they're in Philly and I'm in Atlanta. My older brother Jack is a lawyer in Philly. He watches after Mom since Dad died a few years ago. Steve, the youngest, is in college this year. We keep in touch. Actually, I've been gone from home since I was eighteen."

"Why? It sounds as though you had a marvelously happy family life."

"Oh, yes," Charly said enthusiastically. "Happy but poor. By then my folks were struggling to put Jack through law school. So, I went to work and college at the same time. After graduation, I was lucky enough to get a job with the government in D.C. I worked there for six years until I was transferred to the Bureau of Land Management office in Atlanta four months ago. End, story of my life."

"Aw, and it was so intriguing, too. You were just getting to the part I liked best."

Charly raised her eyebrows. "The part where you come into the story?"

"Naw, the part about your job in Atlanta. Do you like it?" It was a loaded question.

She narrowed her eyes and stopped, arms akimbo. "If

you're expecting a confession about how I hate my job, sorry to disappoint you. It's a good position, and I like it." Her emphatic tone hid her disillusionment with the job and disagreements with her boss, Lewis. Nor did she mention that Lewis wanted to be her lover. That complication was far away as she stood next to Noah, hidden deep in the Smoky Mountains.

He draped his arm around her shoulder affectionately. "Oh, no, Charly. I wasn't looking for a confession. I just wondered if you would quit the rat race and move to the mountains with me."

"Sounds like heaven," she murmured, knowing that deep inside she meant it. "But how would we live? On love?"

He reached around her neck and drew her face close to his. "Hmmm, I'm for that." His kiss was sweet and tender, then he turned and led her on through the woods.

"Enough of my fascinating life. It's time for your exposé," she encouraged.

They walked awhile before Noah spoke, surprising her with stories of his aristocratic Southern family.

"My sister, Missy, and I went to the best prep schools in North Carolina. Fine education, but dull."

"A preppy? You?" Charly hooted with delight. She grabbed his arms and examined him thoroughly, her eyes lingering on the dark beard. "Somehow I never imagined you, of all people, a preppy! A hillbilly, maybe. But not a—"

"Southern is not 'preppy.' Eastern is 'preppy.' " He glared at her.

"Yes, Noah. Anything you say." She acquiesed, grinning delightedly at him. Here was more teasing material— later.

"Do you want to hear this or not?"

"Of course I do. You were just getting to the interesting part." She turned and continued walking.

"If you think that's interesting, wait till you hear this. I even went to The Citadel, military college! While the rest of the world was breaking away, I was marching. God—I hated it! And my dad for sending me."

Charly was appalled at the thought of one's life being so planned. "Did you have to go?"

He shook his head. "There were no alternatives. Missy and I had certain family traditions to uphold. We were groomed to carry on the family name. We spent summers at the Outer Banks' seashore and Sapphire Valley."

"Sapphire Valley?"

"It's a beautiful old resort hotel. There were supervised children's activities to keep us occupied. We were instructed in tennis, golf, horseback riding, and gold mining."

"Gold mining? You're putting me on!"

"Gold mining, yes! Didn't you know that the first gold in the U.S. was discovered in North Carolina? Where have you been all your life, city girl!"

"Well, not looking for gold in North Carolina, that's for sure!" Charly laughed.

"You missed a lot. As a kid, I used to think I'd discover gold in some obscure creek and be rich. Panning for gold was my favorite pastime."

Charly sniffed indignantly. "Sounds to me like you were rich enough."

Noah shrugged and stuffed his hands in his pockets. "Probably. Although I didn't know it. All of my friends lived as I did. I didn't have much personal money. We were just quite busy all the time. I thought everyone spent winter vacations in Ashville or Gatlinburg."

Charly sighed. "What a glorious life you had."

Noah ambled off the path, stepping over tree stumps and roots until he found just the right grassy spot to sit. Charly joined him.

"Not really. My mother drank a lot. Unhappy, I suppose. My sister and I stuck together during that period."

Charly shook her thick hair and let it flow down her back. "Are you and Missy still close?"

He shook his head. "Just friends. When I graduated from The Citadel, I had some hell raising to do. So I spent a few years traveling and getting the hell knocked out of me—one way or another. I rode a rodeo circuit for a while through the West and Canada. That was some experience." He chuckled at some private remembrance. "I was in Alberta, Canada, when they finally reached me that my parents had been killed in a plane crash in the Bahamas."

Charly looked up sharply. What a jolt in the glorious life. Noah was staring through the trees as he talked. She decided not to interrupt with sympathetic comments. Not now.

"So at twenty-five I took the reins of the second largest furniture manufacturing plant in the South. For the first time in my life I worked. And did I ever work! I knew nothing about the business and had to start from scratch."

"Why did you leave it?" Charly asked with trepidation.

"Actually, that's when my glorious life began. I managed to get the business under control, made Missy's husband a partner, and married my high-school sweetheart. By then both Vera and I were around thirty and wanted to start our family as soon as possible. So we had Noah Wade Van Horn the Fourth. Within two years they were both dead. So was the meaning of my life."

"Noah . . ." Charly's voice was gentle as she scooted closer to him and slipped her hand in his.

"So I escaped to the only refuge I knew—these mountains. Here I've found a renewal for my life and strength to continue."

Charly moved to her knees and wrapped her arms around him, cradling his head gently against her breast. "Oh, Noah," she murmured. "I'm sorry about your family—your child . . ." Tears filled her eyes as she empathized with the pain he must have experienced.

105

But he pushed her away, his blue eyes as intense and fierce as his voice. "Don't sympathize or mourn for me, Charly. I've done enough of that already. I've wallowed long enough in my own sorrow and depression. I'm beyond that now. It's a part of my past and I won't go back. I have found new meaning in life—and you have given me new joy. From the moment I saw you with your damn car trouble and when you trooped in covered with mud, I knew that my life had been invaded. No more escaping." He pulled her down to his level and kissed her nose. "But it's been a nice invasion."

Charly smiled through her tears. "What else can you say to me? I'm still here—invading your privacy. But what about when I leave?" She moved away and leaned against the trunk of a giant oak tree that spread its arms over their moss-covered glen.

"What about it?"

"I guess the proof of our . . . relationship . . . will be then." She was scared of the thought, afraid to say it aloud. Her constant fear was that when she left the mountain, she would never see Noah Van Horn III again.

"I guess." Noah lay back on the green mossy bed, using her lap for a pillow. His discerning blue eyes searched for answers in the multitude of tree branches above them and beyond.

Charly ran her fingers through his raven-black hair, relishing the touch. Her other hand lay casually on his muscular chest, tracing small shapes in the hairs.

He shuddered and turned to her, reaching up to cup her breast. "Come here, Charly. I need you . . . want you close. I need you now . . ."

Eagerly, she came to him, burying her face against his chest, clinging tightly to his warmth. The musty smell of the moss-covered earth beneath her mingled with the fresh pine's fragrance, and Charly thought the forest floor was a lovely, natural place to make love. Her passion soared

106

to the heights of the trees above her as Noah caressed her, matching her fervor with his own. Their lovemaking was intense and extravagant, an almost desperate attempt to perpetuate what they feared they would lose. It was as if they sensed this was the last time they would make love— and they lay gratefully, fearfully in each other's arms, trembling at the thought of parting.

Their love was now visible to the world—the trees, the animals, the aged mountains. It was hidden no more. And Charly wanted to shout it to the universe—*I love you, Noah*. But she didn't. She just held him, hiding her tears of joy and passion, hoping she would never, never lose him.

It wasn't the last time Charly and Noah made love. There were other days—and nights. But Charly was staying on borrowed time, and they both knew it. There were no solutions, no offers of relinquishment, no declarations. They just enjoyed the time they had with each other and didn't talk of her leaving.

There were times when Noah or Charly felt entirely content being alone. It was a comfortable feeling, for there was a sense of security between them. Noah had gone off by himself earlier one day and Charly made her way around the clearing, searching purposefully for him. The early morning sun revealed where Noah had secluded himself, and Charly made her way toward him.

"A-ha! Thought you could hide from me, eh? What are you doing up at this hour?"

"Shhh . . ." He held his hand up to stop her, and Charly hushed and eased slowly to the grassy knoll where Noah sat. There, not ten feet away, was a wild, brown rabbit with big ears and a twitching nose. Noah sketched him with quick, sweeping strokes. The light swishing scrawl of the pencil moving across the paper was the only sound they heard, as the forest dominated their presence. Suddenly something spooked the little animal, and he was gone.

Noah and Charly looked at each other, disappointed at his brief debut. Then Noah laughed. "Damn crazy rabbit. Doesn't know when he's in good company!"

"Let me see your drawing," Charly commented, examining the sketches. "Hmmm—not bad, Noah."

He cocked his head, assessing his work. "No. And not good, either. Except for the ears that are too long, the back that's too humped, and the legs that are out of proportion —oh, and the crooked nose—he's perfect!"

"Hey! He's kind of like you, Noah!" Charly teased, and pinched his nose.

Instantly, they were rolling together in the grass, shrieking, wrestling, laughing, kissing . . .

"I meant the 'perfect' part—honestly, Noah! Perfect!" Charly giggled as Noah pinned her arms above her head and kissed her soundly.

"Hmmm—that *was* perfect." He smiled when he finally moved from her willing lips. "Perfect, but not complete. Let's make it complete."

But Charly struggled to be free. "Let me go, Noah. We have to do something for Walt."

"What?"

"Let me up, and I'll tell you," she sputtered, straightening her white blouse and brushing debris from her shoulders. "This is the first time I've dressed in decent clothes in days."

"Are you saying you don't like my clothes?"

"No—yes!" More giggles. "But mine do fit me better. I'm trying to look nice, and you roll me on the ground!"

He grinned at her slyly. "You should be used to it by now. That's the way with us mountain men. Actually, you didn't have to go to all the trouble of putting on decent clothes for me, Charly. I like you in nothing!"

She ignored his teasing remarks and continued to fuss. "I hope I didn't get grass stains on this blouse!"

He inspected her flagrantly, his hand roving over her, lingering on her shoulder. "This does fit you better. I like it!"

"Do you want to hear what Walt wants?"

"No—yes, go ahead." It was hard for him to be serious. Obviously this would be another laugh-filled episode in Charly's mountain fantasy.

"He wants us to go over to the Crismans', wherever they live. Something about trading."

"Sure," Noah agreed, and he began to gather the scattered sketch papers. "We exchange honey and vegetables for eggs and meat and . . . wine."

"Bartering?"

"Yep. It's always been a part of the mountain way. You'll enjoy meeting our neighbors, Ralph and Helga Crisman. And they're just a healthy six-mile hike away." They started for the cabin.

Charly stared incredulously. "*Six* miles?"

"Um-hum. One way."

"Twelve miles in one day? You've got to be kidding me, Noah!"

"Nope. We can't take the truck because there aren't any roads. But you'll love it. It's a nice trip—what a beautiful view from the top! Come on!"

"*Mountain* top? Do you mean we're not on top now?"

Noah turned to her and there was a special glow of appreciation in his deep-blue eyes. "Oh, no, Charly! We're all surrounded here with thick woodlands. You have to climb into the open—on top—before you can see the real beauty."

So both Noah and Charly loaded backpacks full of "barter" and set off on the six-mile hike to Walt's neighbors. Noah was in high spirits, even breaking into song at

109

one point, as the morning sun rose high to humor them and warm their backs.

Charly felt as though she were removed from herself, watching her image go through the paces of being back in time at least a hundred years. In the modern days of jets and space flights and computers, she and Noah were hiking six miles over rugged terrain to the nearest humans. And no one knew where she was. She felt far removed from civilization. It was almost—*almost*—unbelievable.

By the time they arrived at the Crismans' mountain home, Charly was well aware that she had hiked six miles through the rugged Smokies. She slumped exhaustedly on the old porch and gulped the marvelously wet iced tea that Helga offered. She and Noah listened respectfully as first Helga, then Ralph talked nonstop to their first visitors in days.

The old couple insisted that their guests stay and eat. Charly admitted to being starved and offered to help Helga prepare a lunch. The meal they set on the table would have fed six field hands! Charly sat amazed as they all dug in, as if they hadn't eaten in days. There were two kinds of meat, four vegetables, two huge pans of corn bread, and chocolate pie with a beautiful five-inch meringue!

As Helga started to clean the table, Charly murmured to Noah, "Many more lunches like this and you can just roll me off the mountain."

He smiled appreciatively toward Helga. "It was delicious, wasn't it?" Then, to Charly: "I didn't see you holding back! I believe you tried everything!"

Charly smiled sweetly and muttered through her teeth, "I didn't want to hurt her feelings."

They helped clean the kitchen, took a quick tour of the small farm, completed the bartering, and bid the Crismans *adieu*. After all, they had another six-mile trip ahead of them.

"Let's go back a different way. There's a beautiful waterfall I want you to see," Noah said, leading the way.

Charly shook her head wearily, thinking of the miles she had yet to cover. "Y'know, a helicopter could take us home in ten minutes." She dreaded the long hike back, and it was obvious in her lack of enthusiasm.

Noah turned and looked curiously at her for a moment. "A helicopter could take you out of these mountains in ten minutes," he commented tersely.

She caught his sharp eyes for a moment, then looked away. "But, then we'd miss the beautiful waterfall, wouldn't we?" she asked weakly.

His hand gently turned her face toward him again. "It won't be long, Charly. You know that. It's been nine days. The rain has stopped . . ."

"Noah, please! I don't want to think about it. Not yet. I'm not ready to . . ."

"Yes, you are, Charly. I think you are." Abruptly, Noah turned his back and continued along the tree-lined path.

Charly followed, brooding and silent. She knew—fearfully—that he was right. That one day—soon—their odyssey would come to an end. *Then* what?

"Look, Charly," Noah whispered, and pointed toward a small group of deer who looked at them solemnly with large round eyes, then bounded away.

Charly stared, amazed. But it wasn't the deer that drew her curiosity.

"Noah—"

He gazed in the direction where she pointed, but didn't answer her.

"What's that?" She gaped at the huge contraption nestled among the trees beyond where the deer had stood.

"It's what you think," he confirmed, shrugging unconcernedly.

111

"A . . . a whiskey still?" Charly whispered, suddenly apprehensive of their proximity.

He nodded, then turned to continue the trek. "Moonshine. Come on, Charly. It wouldn't be wise for a government official such as you to be caught here."

"My God! Noah! Do you realize—"

"I do! Come on, Charly. I hope you'll forget about this." His tone was terse.

Charly followed, knowing that she wouldn't forget about it, but not quite sure what, if anything, she would do about it. Once again she felt distinctly as though she had been plummeted back in time to another world. Noah's world.

Charly's mind whirled wildly. How long would she stay—should she stay—in the cabin? How in hell would she explain it? Did Noah—or Walt—have anything to do with the illegal whiskey still? After his comments today, was Noah ready for her to leave? Did he dread it as she did? Would he beg her to stay? Would he—oh, God—go with her? Did Noah love her? Or was the love one-sided? *I love you, Noah! Can't you see that?*

"There!" Noah's voice interrupted her confusion. It rose above the loud rush of water as he pointed out the lovely waterfall. "It falls in three levels. Come on. Let's hike down to the final pool." He began the descent through the thick underbrush.

With considerable assistance and effort, Charly finally emerged onto the floor of the narrow, hidden ravine, where the final plunge of the waterfall formed a deep, circular pool. The main rush of the water crashed above them, scattering fine, misty spray everywhere. It was a lovely, enchanted place. Another fantasy in her odyssey.

Charly couldn't resist. The boots she had borrowed from Walt were off in a flash, as well as her backpack. She took one look at the emerald pool framed with gray boul-

112

ders, sprinkled with silvery mist, hidden from the world, and knew she had to be a part of it.

"Ohhh, it's beautiful, Noah! The water is so inviting—I want to go in!"

Noah shrugged. "Go ahead and wade."

"No . . . I mean I want to swim in it!" Charly was excited at the thought.

He smiled knowingly. "Charly, it's very cold . . ."

"Hell, I'm used to cold water after all those awful showers at the cabin! Come on, Noah! Come in with me!"

Slowly, he smiled. "There's only one way to go, Charly. In the buff!"

She looked at him for a moment, then met his challenge with a devilish grin. "I'll beat you in!"

Impatiently, feverishly, they stripped. Charly was determined to be the first one into the beautiful water.

Noah's low tone was intended for another warning, but it only served to spur her faster. "Charly, this water is *ice* cold. Are you sure . . ."

"Yes, I'm sure! It's beautiful, and I'm hot from all this damn hiking! It's just too tempting to pass up!" She laid her clothes carefully on the pack and hesitated only a moment before plunging, nude, into the misty, sunlit pool.

Noah laughed as Charly shrieked and howled when the icy water immediately chilled her hot body and practically took her breath away in the process.

"Oh—oh, my God! This is freezing! Damn—it's cold!" she gasped at him from where she treaded water in the deep center of the pool. Then she smiled and teased him sweetly, "Come on in, Noah, the water's fine! Once you get used to it—" Her words were cut short by her chattering teeth, but she managed a smile.

Noah looked at her skeptically, for he knew the truth. He hesitated on the bank, for he knew the full impact of the icy water and tried to delay it as long as possible.

He climbed onto a boulder and Charly admired his

113

muscular, masculine form as he stood poised. But she wasn't about to risk that he wouldn't join her. "You'd better get in here—or I'm coming after you!" she yelled, wondering how she would ever force him to do anything.

With a shout that echoed off the rocks above them, Noah dove in and swam swiftly through the water. He stroked evenly across the pool, then back to where Charly huddled on an underwater rock.

"You have to move around, Charly. Get the circulation going or icicles will form . . ." He grinned and clasped both of her breasts teasingly.

Together they swam a few laps, touching, teasing, chasing each other in the breathtakingly cold water.

"I . . . I think I've had enough, Noah," Charly finally admitted through chattering teeth.

"Thank God—I thought you'd never want to get out! I'm afraid my masculinity is ruined for life!" He pushed her through the water toward the bank.

They sat in the evening sun, drying each other with Noah's shirt, rubbing vigorously to revive their chilled senses. Soon their efforts gave way to soothing caresses and gentle touches that aroused passions. Noah couldn't resist kissing Charly until her lips parted with willing desire and her chilled skin tingled with warm passion. Charly wrapped her arms around his neck and clung to him, molding her lithe figure to his muscular frame. She enjoyed the warmth that radiated from him and wriggled with pleasure.

"It's so warm here with you. Feels so good," she murmured against his cheek as he lifted her off the ground and carried her to a soft, grassy spot. Her feet touched the cushioned earth and he reached to loosen her grip on him.

"Let go, Charly. I'll spread my shirt." Clumsily he made a crude bed for them. Then he turned to her, his passion strong and virile. "Come here, little Wildcat."

Eagerly she knelt on the shirt beside Noah. He ran his

hand along her thigh and pulled her to him, igniting the flame that burned in her.

"I'm yours, Noah. Just yours—for always," she murmured in his ear.

He answered in a hoarse whisper. "Don't say 'always.' Right now. Be mine *now.*"

She shuddered and surrendered her love to this man who wanted her now, but not forever. Or so he said.

But Charly wasn't like that. The man who elicited such wonderful heights of emotion—delight, excitement, passion—would always have her love. She was convinced of this and gave to him freely.

Later, as they lay in each other's arms, she stroked his chest and murmured, "I can assure you of one thing, Noah."

"What's that?" His voice was still low and dreamy.

"You weren't ruined for life by that ice water! Maybe stimulated!" They chuckled and snuggled together, gathering warmth from each other.

"We'd better start back soon, Charly. It's getting late."

"I know. But I hate to leave this spot—and you. I may just stay here forever and never go back to civilization!" Her voice was full of love.

His hand titillated her creamy breasts as he talked. "Oh? You love those cold showers, eh?"

"Hardly! Maybe I do miss civilization and my nice, warm scented bath."

His hand trailed to her face, around her lips, tracing their shape. "Do you remember when you fought me to let you go? Wasn't too many days ago."

She smiled sheepishly. "I know—but that was before . . ."

"Don't make any commitments now, Charly. Just enjoy the present." His fingers stroked her flat stomach.

"Is that what you're doing, Noah? Just enjoying the present?"

He smiled and nuzzled her ear. "You bet I am. Let's get dressed, Charly. We need to start back before dark."

They dressed quietly, regretfully. Noah tied the wet shirt around his waist and led the way over the remaining mile to the cabin. It had been one of those exhaustingly perfect days. Charly felt so at ease, so totally wonderful with Noah, she couldn't imagine leaving him. Oh, how she wished they could be together forever. Did he really mean it the time he had said, "Quit the rat race and move to the mountains with me?" Could she really do that? Would she?

As they approached the clearing where the old cabin stood, the soft silence of their forest world was interrupted by the unmistakable drone of a vehicle's motor.

CHAPTER EIGHT

Charly stood numbly as Lewis Daniel embraced her fervently, backpack and all. He held her at arm's length and examined her, his eyes traveling over her five-foot, four-inch frame. He ogled at her braless mien, where her firm-shaped nipples were outlined naturally, tantalizing him.

Charly's cheeks were pink, her face slightly flushed. She was hot and grimy, her clothes less than tidy after the twelve-mile hike. Her chestnut hair hung loosely curled around her shoulders, the way it had dried after her dip in the mountain stream. Was that a leaf entangled in a tousled wave? She presented an unsophisticated, vulnerable appearance, as opposed to her usual polish and grace. Yet Charly's natural beauty was never more obvious.

A band of tiny beads of sweat was barely visible across Lewis's forehead as he exclaimed, "Charly, have you been here all this time? I've been worried sick about you! I can't believe this has happened to you! Are you all right?" There was emphasis on the "all right" and Charly knew that Lewis meant more than the words implied. He hadn't changed.

There seemed to be a crowd of men, all talking and exchanging greetings. Walt and Noah shook hands with Lewis, then someone else. Charly turned her attention from Lewis and recognized the forest ranger, Crockett. He had been kind enough to drive Lewis up that "dangerous" road to rescue her. *Rescue?* Crockett said something of assurance to Lewis about being confident all along that Charly would be all right. He had known Walter Simms a long time and . . .

Lewis wrapped his arms around her again, and she was engulfed with the fragrance of his expensive cologne. Suddenly it was overpoweringly unpleasant, and she pushed him away from her. Charly was accustomed to Noah's fresh, natural smell, and any other was now repulsive.

Lewis was still the same intense, powerful person. In a low voice he asked urgently, "Charly, are you really *all right?* I mean . . . have you been held here against your will . . . or has anything *else* happened to you that I should know? Have you been here, in this hovel, the entire two weeks?" He couldn't hide the exasperation in his voice.

"It's only been nine days, Lewis." Somehow, it sounded so short to her now.

His voice was urgent as he rushed to explain. "I would have been here sooner, Charly—you know that—but I was in D.C. all last week. Hell, I didn't even know you hadn't reported in until Monday. We wasted two days trying to reach you at the Azalea Inn. Lovely place. They didn't know anything about you. Same with the dumb bastards in the office. Finally, I knew I had to come find you myself. Damn! I'm glad to see you!"

There was a definite message in his story of "how and why" and Charly detected it immediately. She was to thank him for "rescuing" her, but she just couldn't bring herself to do it.

Instead she smiled reassuringly at him. "I'm fine, Lewis. I've just been stranded up here because of the rain. Didn't you pass my car on the way? It's been mired in the mud since the first day. Walter Simms and . . . Noah . . . have been very nice. They've taken good care of me." She felt good that she hadn't let Lewis intimidate her. But why didn't Noah speak up? Where was he, anyway?

Lewis still talked the same, but he looked haggard. His

dark hair, tinged with gray at the temples, was slightly awry from the rough trip up the mountain, but he was impeccably dressed in brown slacks and expensive beige sport shirt. His face, tanned from every-Friday-afternoon golf matches, was clean-shaven and lean, edged with worry lines. He ran the office operations with an iron hand, and Charly had caused ripples since her arrival. He was dedicated to another tactic for ruling her. She shuddered at the thought.

She stood, as if in a daze, while the men talked. She was vaguely aware that her backpack had been removed and Noah wasn't beside her anymore. She looked around for him, but he wasn't to be seen.

The arm around her shoulder squeezed tightly to get her attention, and Lewis's commanding voice directed her, "Get your things, honey, and let's go. Mr. Crockett wants to get off this mountain before dark. And I *know* you don't want to spend another night in this place."

Another night? Just one more night . . .

Charly nodded and a strange, faraway voice said, "Let me get my purse."

In the big room Noah stood wide-legged with his back to her, looking intently out the back door. What is he thinking? she wondered. Why doesn't he let me know? Why doesn't he stop me? He would, if only . . . if only . . . A small sob welled up within her.

Charly allowed her gaze to leave Noah's broad back and drift about the room, conjuring memories of nights curled by the fireplace, cutting Noah's hair, drying his back, cooking together, making love in the small book-filled bedroom. Her eyes returned to Noah and the muscular back she had rubbed and caressed. It angered her that he wouldn't look at her, talk to her.

"Noah, it's time to go. I . . . I have to leave now." Her voice was slightly shaky and she moved across the dark room to stand close to him.

He turned to her then, arms folded across his chest, dark blue eyes interposing and nonemotional. It was as if he dared her to love him.

He said nothing, so she stammered, "I . . . I don't want to . . . to leave you."

He shrugged. His voice was low, but steady. "But you must go, Charly. You know that. And I understand."

Charly was beside herself! "You sound as though you don't even care!" Damn him! His laissez-faire attitude was infuriating!

His eyes met hers steadily. "Oh, I care. You have renewed the joy in my life, Charly. I wish our little odyssey could last forever. But we both know that's impossible. Oh, yes, I do care. But it's no use. There is nothing I—or you—can do about it."

Was there a touch of emotion, concern . . . oh, God, *love* . . . in his tone? Charly's hopes rose. "Then will you come back with me, Noah? Will you leave this place? We can make it together. I know we can."

He hesitated and took a deep breath. A low, mocking chuckle escaped with his first words. "Back to 'civilization'? No, Charly. I won't leave Walt now. At least, not for long. My responsibilities are here. You know that."

In that second her hopes were dashed. All her dreaming, hoping, loving were for naught. "Nothing we can do about it"! The words would haunt her. Nothing! It's all for nothing! A sob caught inside Charly's throat, almost choking her, for she now realized that, indeed, they were parting. Her old fear of never seeing him again—never loving him—returned to smother her. Defensively, she explained, "I have responsibilities, too. My job . . . ."

"I know, Charly. I knew all along that you would leave. You have to go, and I understand that. I have to stay. I hope *you* understand." His voice was gentle.

Understand? To hell with understanding! Charly didn't want understanding and lashed at him bitterly. "So, you

120

have enjoyed our little fling while it lasted. Just like you said earlier in the week. And now it's 'Good-bye and good luck.' Just like that!"

Noah looked at her for a long moment, assessing her anger, deciding to allow it. It made the parting so much easier for both of them. "You have a job to do, Charly. So do I," he answered quietly.

She grabbed her purse, her only personal possession in the cabin for nearly two weeks. "Well, you don't have to worry about my job, Noah. I'll ask to be removed from this case. I'm not a disinterested party anymore. I'm trying to be, but I'm not."

The jeep horn blasted loudly and impatiently, reminding them that Lewis and the "civilized" world awaited her. Charly slipped her feet out of Walt's clumsy boots and walked purposely over to Noah. She touched his hard chest and stood on tiptoe to kiss him one last time. It was a dry, unresponsive kiss—just lips touching, brushed by a velvet beard, then gone.

"Good-bye, Noah," she whispered.

She padded barefooted out the door and hugged Walt quickly on the porch. "Thanks for everything, Walt. I'll . . . I'll try to help you." Her voice was husky and strained.

The old man stared at her intently, his blue eyes shining defiantly. "For a city gal, you did pretty good up here. And you fix good vegetable soup—for a city gal."

It was the closest he would come to a compliment. Charly smiled her appreciation and left the cabin, not knowing what, if anything, she could do to help this old man—not knowing if she would ever see Noah again.

She crawled into the jeep, barefooted and bedraggled, and slumped unhappily into the seat beside Mr. Crockett. He shifted gears and the vehicle jostled roughly away. Charly purposely didn't meet Lewis's eyes, fearing her expression would show her true feelings. She was very close to tears and didn't want these men to see her crying. They might misunderstand.

Noah watched darkly from the window as Charly climbed into the vehicle and it started to roll away. He stood unblinking as Lewis draped his arms securely around Charly and kissed her. She didn't resist the affection Lewis lavished on her and remained in his encircling arms until the jeep rolled out of sight down the mountain road. Noah stalked outside then, letting the door slam behind him, jerking off the binding shirt as he moved. His muscles flourished as he raised the ax high overhead and brought it crashing down with all his might, again and again, until it was so dark that he couldn't see the pile of wood he had chopped. Then he lit a kerosene lantern and chopped until exhaustion overtook him and he dragged his spent body to the ice-cold shower.

Charly reclined against the back of her large old tub, relishing the luxuriant feeling of the warm water lapping over her sensitive skin. The millions of bubbles caught the various colors from the small candle that glowed on her vanity and clustered in pinks and violets and yellows around her legs, breasts, and shoulders. How much of this self-indulgence would it take to obliterate those nine days she spent without what she considered the necessities of life. She was exhausted after the long trip back to Atlanta. She and Lewis had driven relentlessly through the night, finally catching a midnight flight from Knoxville to Atlanta. Lewis had hovered, and Charly had let him. She functioned in a shocked state. But he understood. He had assured her of that. But he didn't—not really. Oh, God— did *she*? Was it a dream?

Returning to Atlanta and seeing her familiar belongings had jolted Charly back to the realities of her life. After living in the simple cabin, the modest apartment Charly called her own was such a welcome sight. The long east

122

window, with its glass étagère full of plants, was the city version of her two-week odyssey close to nature. Thank goodness Mrs. Kline, her landlady, had kept them watered and alive. And her cat, Mitts. He sat behind the elephant ears and occasionally swatted a leaf, refusing to come to her right away.

"Dumb cat." She fussed. She unloaded the small suitcase and cosmetic case—neither of which had been touched during her entire trip—that she had taken from the trunk of her abandoned car.

Charly looked in the mirror at her miserable appearance. The natural face, free of makeup, the windblown hair, a slight tan on her nose, and an unmistakably healthy glow to her cheeks contrasted sharply with her eyes. Oh, God, those eyes! They were red-rimmed, dark-hollowed reminders of the pain she felt inside.

She pinched her pink cheeks. "Maybe there was something good for me in all that—maybe," she mumbled, as she began to run warm water into the marvelous old tub. It was an ancient one with legs and deep enough to cover her body with water—almost.

Without delay, Charly had stripped off her bedraggled clothes and stepped into the shallow water. She settled in the near-empty tub and closed her eyes, letting the warm water creep slowly around her aching body. All she wanted to do was to wash away the entire mountain experience —as if that were possible.

Oddly, she now lived in the lap of luxury just because she had hot running water, a flushable commode, electricity, and a stove that heated immediately without hauling wood to it. Thank God, she was home!

And no more cold showers! Actually, Charly thought she would never get enough of her warm, fragrant, relaxing baths. Oh, she had really missed this. She opened her eyes and the candle's glow flickered light shadows on the wall. The lemony scent permeated the room. Suddenly, she shut her eyes tightly, pinching the vision of Noah by the fireplace, making love to her with his eyes. She heaved a sigh. Oh, when would he go away?

Charly's favorite Nancy Wilson records filled the background with soft, romantic sounds. It was definitely more pleasant than a harmonica! Enormously so! Charly swayed slightly to the hypnotic beat, trying not to slosh her bath water on the carpeted floor. *Oh, yes . . . this is the life . . . so nice . . .*

But there was one memory that her easy, comfortable life-style couldn't obliterate. Noah. Noah Van Horn. Were those two weeks in the rugged mountain cabin a dream? But life there was harsh. It wasn't the sort of place one dreamed of. Was Noah her fantasy? He had never declared his love. Never.

Charly ran her hand over her body, slick from the bubbles and oil. Shuddering, she recalled his caress and knew he was real. Brief, but real. She had never responded to anyone like she had to Noah. His touch warmed her, thrilled her, tore at her reason, intensified her passion. Suddenly, she missed him terribly, longed for his gentle hands on her, craved his lean, dark body next to hers.

Tormented in her longed-for tub, with scented candles and ever-relaxing music, there was nothing strong enough to make her forget her love. There was no escaping! Great tears welled up in her eyes as she fought the image of his face in her mind. She saw him teasing her, loving her, standing immobile for the last passionless kiss, telling her to go with his eyes. And she cried—great, heaving sobs for the first time since she left the humble little cabin and Noah.

Only now did she realize the full impact of her experience. She had fallen ridiculously, hopelessly in love with a stranger who didn't return her love. And she would never see—or touch—Noah Van Horn again.

* * *

Charly put her hands on the mahogany desk before her and leaned on them. Her brown eyes snapped furiously at Lewis. "I told you before. I want to be taken off this case! In fact, I insist on it!"

Lewis leaned back in his swivel chair and kept his voice calm. "And I told you, Charly, I don't think that's necessary. I'll assign it to Ben if you want. But I want you to work with him on it."

"But why? I've told you everything I know about it. And, after a trip up there, I failed to come back with enough evidence . . ."

Lewis's steady, calm voice instructed her. "Please sit down, Charly. Now, I know that entire episode has left you depressed and uptight. That's to be expected, honey. You've been through a bad experience and I won't send you back. You don't have to worry about that. But I'm not giving up on the case just because you're ready to drop it. We'll work with you to help you finish it."

Charly sat on the edge of the chair opposite Lewis. She gazed out the window of his spacious office, which afforded a lovely view of Atlanta from the tenth floor. The city sparkled with fall sunshine and bustled with the noisy business of the day. She used to enjoy it—thrive on the activity of the city, thrill to be a part of it. But now it annoyed her. It was too loud, and fast—maybe she just needed to get away for a while. But she'd been away . . .

" . . . Charly, you're not listening. I think you know a lot more about this case than you're telling. For instance, what is Van Horn doing up there? You haven't explained his presence to my satisfaction at all . . ."

Charly twisted her hands nervously. "I told you, Lewis, I don't know! I just don't . . ."

"You were with him the day we arrived. What were you two doing together? Where had you been? What did you

125

see deep in those mountains?" His voice was sinister and driving.

"Don't grill me as if I were a criminal, Lewis. I don't have to answer that!"

Damn! She'd been impossible lately! "I'm just trying to ascertain some facts, Charly. I think you're holding back info that's pertinent to the case. This lifetime-lease case is important. And, Charly, I intend to find out about that situation if I have to send someone else back up there. I think even more is going on than we suspected—and you may know about it! My God! You spent almost two weeks up there! You *have* to know more about the old man's life-style than you're telling!" Lewis's voice was vicious.

Charly spread her hands. "I only know that an old man lives up there and he deserves to continue to live on his property until he dies, according to his lease."

Lewis's wicked golden eyes narrowed. "You sound like you've switched allegiances, Charly. Two weeks with the enemy and the prisoner becomes sympathetic to his cause."

Charly's voice rose shrilly. "I was not there two weeks! I was only there nine days! And they—he—is *not* an enemy! Walter Simms is a nice, trusting old man who is just trying to live and let live. And what is this enemy bit? You're not still in the army, y'know! I wasn't a prisoner!"

"Then why didn't you leave?"

"I . . . I couldn't! You saw my car! It was a total loss. Mr. Crockett had to hire someone to tow it away! You know I couldn't leave! My papers and everything were stuck in the car." She didn't tell him that she and Noah had hiked twelve miles the day Lewis arrived. In actuality, she could have hiked off the mountain and halfway to town. But then, she didn't want to leave. She only wanted to be with Noah. She even threatened never to go back to civilization. So why *had* she? She had asked herself that a million times already. Her head reeled with the thought, but Lewis's staccato-paced words snapped her back.

"What do you know about Van Horn?"

"Nothing!" Her answer was too quick, too severe.

"Nothing? *You* were with him . . . hiking, did you say? Bartering with neighbors? Come on, Charly. What *is* Van Horn doing there?"

She looked Lewis in the eye and shrugged. "He's a friend of Walt's. He stopped by to help Walt." She couldn't believe she was being so calm while talking about Noah.

"And you just went along for the walk."

Charly glared at him. He was setting her up, and she knew it. Slowly, she answered. "Something like that. I can tell you one thing for sure, Lewis. I will report on the simple mountain life of Walter Simms of Simms Hollow, North Carolina. But I won't sign a derogatory report on him, because now, after being there, I feel that he is not harming anything or anybody by living there."

"Simple life?" Lewis's laugh was wicked. "I thought we determined there were factors warranting his expulsion before you even made the trip up there. Now, after spending two weeks—excuse me, nine days—up there, you can't tell me one harmful thing the old man's doing. Not shooting animals, not running moonshine . . ."

"Moonshine?" Her eyes widened and she feared betrayal.

"Aw, come on, Charly. Surely you know about that! All of those mountain people brew a little 'shine' and run it occasionally—or regularly! How do you think they make a living?"

"They do not!" Charly was on her feet again. "That's not true! Walt doesn't . . . do that! I swear it!" She tried not to be too emphatic. In her mind, there were already doubts that she could keep up this pressure and not reveal a piece of knowledge that would be used against Simms.

127

Whether the illegal whiskey still she had seen belonged to him or not, if she let it slip that she had even seen one, Lewis would twist the information the way he wanted it.

Lewis walked around the desk and placed his arm around her shoulders. He could feel her quivering inside and knew he was pushing her too far. But maybe now was the time to find out about Charly's relationship with Van Horn. It gnawed at his gut to think what might have taken place between them. Damn! He had to know! Charly denied cognizance of anything about him, but there was tension in the air whenever Van Horn's name was mentioned. Lewis could feel it.

"Calm down, Charly. Come, sit over here." He tried to lead her to the two-seater sofa.

Charly jerked from his grasp. "Get your hands off me," she said, seething. She was different since her trip, all right. He hadn't been able to take her to lunch, much less touch her. He had tried to be patient, but that was wearing thin. He was sure something had occurred between them in the mountains.

Lewis leaned against the heavy desk, looming near her, yet not touching her. The gold flecks in his eyes gleamed menacingly. "All right, Charly. Tell me about Van Horn. What was he doing at the cabin? What do you know about him?"

"Nothing! I told you, I don't know anything about him!"

"Did you know he comes from a very wealthy family in Charlotte? *The* Van Horns, furniture magnates in the South for over a hundred years? Now what would a man like that be doing in the mountains? Living there? He has enough money to buy the whole damn place!"

Charly folded her arms defensively. It helped steady them and hide her shaking hands. Her voice was derisive as she hid her own shock upon learning how much Lewis

128

knew about Noah. "It is public domain, you know. National Forest means anyone can enter, Lewis!"

"I want to know what he was doing with *you!* Is he living in that cabin? Did you live with him for two weeks, Charly?"

Her eyes narrowed and she worked to keep her voice steady. "I think our conversation is finished, Lewis! I won't answer any more of your stupid questions! And I won't file or sign a derogatory report on this case. The only way you'll get any help from me is to take me off the case!" She wheeled toward the door, but before she reached the handle, Lewis grabbed her arm, his fingers digging through her blazer and into her skin.

"I am not relieving you from this case, Charly. The inquisition will continue. Right now Mr. Van Horn is being investigated. Soon we'll know all about him, and you won't be able to hide what you know any longer. I'm trusting that you will still come around."

"Don't hold your venomous breath, Lewis." Charly snapped her aching arm away from Lewis's grasp and left the office. She was so angry, her entire body shook. And she knew it would be impossible to hold up with much more of this kind of pressure from Lewis. She wasn't sure what she could do about it—would do—but there had to be something.

She flew into her office and slammed the door. Damn him, anyway! He suspected something between her and Noah. If he hadn't cared about her, tried to seduce her, the matter wouldn't bother him at all. He probably wouldn't pursue it. But there was a jealousy apparent— and God knows, there was nothing to be jealous about. Not anymore. What happened between her and Noah had been a fling—she had heard nothing from Noah in the weeks since she had left. It was as if it had never happened. One long, miserable month had passed, and Charly had heard nothing. But what did she expect? Love letters?

Hardly! She knew better! She knew she would never see him again. And it was just as well. But the least she could do was protect Walt. And she would try to do that with all her ability—what wasn't eroded by Lewis.

She was furious that he wouldn't relieve her of the responsibility of the case. There was a purpose in that, and she knew it. He hadn't pressed her on it until now. But she sensed there would be increased pressure as time progressed. Lewis was relentless in getting what he wanted, whether it was a resolved case or personal satisfaction. She knew she was a part of that personal satisfaction he desired. It was still obvious to her, even though she had held him off so far. Lately, she had been downright rude to the man, and still he persisted. She shivered at the thought of Lewis's hands on her. She couldn't even stand his arm lightly around her shoulders. She was haunted by the bearded mountain man's touch—more now than when she had first returned. Memory must do something to enhance the imagination. No one could have been that enticing to her. Surely . . .

Charly fumbled in her desk, drawing out a thick folder full of papers. She had these reports to complete, then there was nothing pressing until next Monday. She could work late and finish them, then call in sick tomorrow. She needed the time off, needed to get her head together. It was getting to be a habit taking Fridays off—three of the last four Fridays had been to "get her head together." It hadn't worked yet. What made her think it would now?

Time. That's what they all said—time will heal the hurt. But so far time had enhanced her hurt. It just meant more time that she hadn't seen him. Oh, damn! What could she do to obliterate Noah from her mind?

CHAPTER NINE

Lewis glanced at the office clock. It read 8:10. He knew it had been dark for several hours, but they had been so busy, they had lost track of the time. He looked across the small conference desk, laden with scattered papers, and smiled. Charly's tousled brown head was bent in intense concentration as she poured over the papers before her. She made notes here and there, checked a long accompanying list, and continued reading, oblivious to Lewis's admiring gaze.

His voice was gentle. "Charly, let's call it quits. I'm beat and I know you are. It's after eight. We can finish this tomorrow."

She looked up and automatically checked the clock, then glanced outside, where the city lights glittered in a sea of darkness. Sighing, she nodded in agreement. Her head felt like a heavy weight. "Let me finish this page. It'll only take a few minutes." She continued her task, not realizing that Lewis still hadn't taken his eyes off her and that they held a special glow.

Lewis smiled with inner satisfaction, his eyes settling on her full breasts, wishing he could get his hands on them. Even with no lipstick and her hair disarrayed, she was attractive . . . alluring . . . sexy. He was taken with her appeal—had been from the time she first came to work for him. Maybe tonight . . .

"It's been a long week, honey. I want you to know how

much I appreciate your working late every night to help me finish this damned project," he complimented her earnestly.

She glanced up and shrugged. "Everyone has put in long hours on it, Lewis. It goes with the job. I just seem to get stuck with the night duty. I'll remember this when I ask for my next raise." Was there a touch of the old Charly—joking, teasing, carefree?

He reached across the table and patted her hand, covering hers while he talked. "Don't worry, Charly. I won't forget. I'm well aware that your efforts have been over and above the call of duty. And now the project is practically finished, thanks to your work tonight. In fact, this calls for a celebration. How about grabbing a bite to eat with me? I'm starved!"

Charly tried not to jerk away from his hand, but his touch jolted through her. She knew she was being overly sensitive. Casually, she started to organize the papers into orderly stacks. What harm would there be in a meal together? She hadn't been out in so long—and Lewis had been nice to her at work. There had been no more confrontations. None. And she, too, was starved . . .

"Sure, Lewis. Sounds great. Give me a few minutes to repair my makeup." She hastened to the ladies' room, then accompanied him eagerly to his car.

The "bite to eat" turned out to be a sumptuous four-course meal at one of Atlanta's finest, taking two hours to eat and accompanied by two kinds of wine. Lewis certainly outdid himself, lavishing Charly with attention and wine. The heavy meal—or was it the wine?—left Charly somewhat lethargic, and she smiled solicitously as Lewis entertained her. He was charming, witty, the proper gentleman. Charly knew she was being pursued, but it was a nice feeling. It had been so long since she had been out with a man, catered to, sought after. She hadn't dated anyone and had remained holed up in her lonely apartment for the past two months, nursing her broken heart. And it had been much too long.

Lewis had let up on his relentless pursuit of her knowledge of the lifetime-lease case. It hadn't been discussed in weeks. She had submitted reports to close the case, but she hadn't heard anything on that. Charly was sure Lewis had received information on the pending investigation of Noah, but it hadn't been mentioned. Charly certainly wasn't going to broach the subject. She was trying her best to forget Noah Van Horn, just as he had forgotten her. And she was sure now that Noah didn't give a damn about their relationship, those lustful days they'd spent together. Nor did he care about her feelings.

She hadn't heard a word from him since the day he'd encouraged her to leave the mountain, saying he understood. Oh, how she hated him for understanding! Oh, God, here she was thinking about him again. Her mind rambled sometimes—beyond her control.

"Charly—hey, Charly! Are you ready to go?" Lewis was leaning anxiously toward her, trying to get her attention. His hand warmly covered hers.

She jerked back to the reality of her location, across from Lewis. "Yes? Oh, yes, Lewis." She smiled wanly and stood so he could drape her tweed blazer around her shoulders.

Lewis kept one arm possessively around her shoulders as they left the restaurant. It was as if he didn't want to let her out of reach. He drove rapidly through the city and halted beside an unfamiliar building. Charly looked at him questioningly.

Calmly, he answered her unasked question by suggesting, "Let's go in to my place and have a drink together, Charly. Maybe some coffee. Or, I have some nice brandy." His expression and tone were casually encouraging, but he didn't rush her. He waited patiently for her answer. He had been so patient for many months now.

She smiled her assent. "Well, maybe just a little brandy. Can you believe that I've never had brandy? But remember, we have to work tomorrow, boss." After she agreed to accompany him, she began to have small doubts. Actually, it was a little risky. She really didn't care if she was with Lewis or not. It could be anyone. Indifference was the way she went through her life these days. But that had to end—someday . . . some night . . .

"Permit me, madam." Lewis was already opening the car door, offering his hand to help her exit the vehicle. Before she knew it, she was inside his apartment, taking the round goblet he handed her. She sniffed the pungent brandy and decided this was going a bit far for someone who happened to like homemade blackberry wine. She smiled to herself and walked around the nice but not entirely elegant room. The decor was distinctly masculine in browns and rusts and dark blues. There was a mixture of old and new furniture, indicating a collection through the years. She wondered briefly if he had ever been married. Funny, she had never asked—never cared. The sofa was old and worn, a nearby brass and glass table shiny and new. Sliding glass doors opened onto a small patio that overlooked the city. The lights formed patterns in the backdrop of blackness and glistened like diamonds on display as cars moved along ribbon streets. Charly turned back to Lewis. She had stalled long enough, gathering her courage.

Lewis stood waiting patiently—oh, so patiently—for her attention. Yes, tonight was the night. He sensed it—felt it . . . He licked his lips in anticipation.

Appropriately, he crossed the space between them. Slowly, his arms went around her and Charly raised her head so that he could kiss her. When his lips touched hers, she involuntarily sucked in her startled breath and tried

134

to step back—away from his lips, his advances. Is this really what she wanted? Not really—not yet! She struggled again, but Lewis seemed prepared for her reaction. He kept his arms securely around her, preventing her escape from his clutches. Wisely, he held himself in check and didn't try to force his kisses on her, for he wanted Charly to come to him willingly. And she was so close. Patience . . .

His voice was thick with passion, and his breath fell in raspy spurts on her face. "Charly . . . Charly. Don't fight me. I won't force you. But I can make it good. I can help you forget him if you'll give me a chance. Let me make you forget him."

Charly gasped audibly and looked at Lewis with wild eyes. He knew! Damn him! He knew about Noah! "I . . . I don't know what you're talking about, Lewis," she managed. She pushed gently on his chest.

"Yes you do, Charly," he cajoled softly. "Your beautiful eyes are those of a woman in love—a woman scorned." He said the word with contempt. "Face it, Charly. The only way you'll forget him is to replace him with someone else—someone better."

Replace Noah? She felt slightly dizzy and rubbed her forehead, pushing again on him. "Oh, Lewis . . . don't— don't rush me. I don't know . . ." She shook her head, puzzled over the turn of events and her own torrid emotions.

Reluctantly, he released her, and Charly stepped back reflexively. She gulped the drink, staring into the glass as if the answers she sought danced inside. The brandy seared her insides, but within moments created a small, growing glow. Help me?

Lewis's voice was low and gentle. "I won't rush you, Charly. I'm here when you need me. Don't forget—when you needed me on the mountain, when you were stranded,

I came for you. I won't leave you, Charly. I'll always be here . . . for you."

His voice was soothing. She liked the things he said. He had rescued her from the mountain and . . . Noah. But he sounded too good. Could she really believe him? Charly drank again, emptying the glass this time, for she wanted to obliterate Noah's memory and . . . what was now happening to her and . . . what she was about to do. *Yes! Help me! Make me forget!* She took a deep breath and a step toward him.

"Make me forget, Lewis. Make me forget tonight. I . . . I don't know why it took so long . . ." She opened her arms to him.

Instantly, Lewis's lean arms were around her, his lips savagely abusing hers, his hands raking over her body. Charly tried to submit completely to the pleasures Lewis had promised. The one thing she wanted in the world was Noah's love. But since she couldn't have it, she would forget him—block out his memory altogether. And Lewis had assured her he would help her do that. He would make her forget. She stifled a sob as he lifted her to the broad sofa, his hands roughly seeking her breasts, fumbling at her blouse buttons. Wildly, she wondered how many others had forgotten their sorrows on Lewis's tattered sofa. His hot groping hands touched the sensitive areas of her breasts, seeking to ignite in Charly the desires that matched his.

Spontaneously, unavoidably, Charly's latent emotions emerged in a single frantic cry. "Noah!"

Immediately, Lewis's ardent motions halted. Damn! Patience, be damned! He wanted her . . . *now!*

In the brief moment of indecision, Charly managed to scramble frantically from the sofa, away from Lewis's grasp. Her brown mane tumbled over part of her frightened face and her blouse hung open, revealing heaving breasts. "No, Lewis! I'm . . . I'm sorry, Lewis. Honest I am! I . . . I just can't! Not now. Not yet. I . . . I hope you understand!" She didn't understand, so why should he? She only knew she couldn't bear his touch. She grasped at her gaping blouse, buttoning it blindly.

Lewis stared at her, anger and frustration written on his tortured face. And she couldn't blame him. She had led him on, then done the unforgivable. But right now all she wanted to do was get away from him. Before he could stop her, she had grabbed her purse and jacket and bolted from the apartment. She emerged almost wildly onto the street, amazed at the amount of traffic at this late hour. The gusty autumn wind chilled her blazing body and she quickly donned her jacket, shivering with emotion as much as coldness. Confused, she started to run along the street, needing only to get home. A car stopped near the curb where she moved and honked at her. Frantically, fearfully, she looked around.

"Taxi, ma'am?"

Gratefully, she nodded and lunged into the cab, spouting off her address without a thought to her safety. All she wanted to do was to get home where she could be alone—alone again!

Charly fumbled for her apartment key, finally managing to unlock the door and breathlessly slip inside. She was shaking like a leaf in a storm. Her ragged emotions were tearing her apart, ravaging her reason. And *he* was the cause! Oh, how she hated him! A sob rose like a suffocating mound in her chest and she wanted to scream. *No! I love you, Noah!* She couldn't even deny it to herself, couldn't escape its binding snare. She was caught in Noah's trap, as helpless as the animals who had made the mistake of getting too close. That's what she had done. She had gotten too close. She had cared too much.

Charly turned toward the welcoming darkness of her small home and gasped, a fearful cry of alarm rising aloud from her open mouth. There, outlined in the dark, loomed the broad-shouldered figure of a man!

The low voice that followed her gasp settled her fears, for she recognized it immediately. "Hey, Wildcat, don't you ever stay at home?"

"Noah? Is it you? Noah!"

Instantly, she flung herself into his arms, clinging to him for dear life, crying tears of disbelief and joy onto his beard and neck. He held her like that until her sobbing hushed, caressing her hair, murmuring soft words. She didn't even wonder where he came from, or why he was there, or how he'd gotten into her apartment. That would come later. Right now she only knew that he was here, holding her. It was like a dream. Yet another dream. But Noah wasn't a dream—she touched him, smelled him, felt his warmth against her. And that's all that mattered.

It was a long time before Charly raised her head from his broad chest. She probably should be mad at him. But she was so glad to see him, she just wanted to cling to him. She felt like the mother who couldn't decide whether to hug or spank her runaway son. Love won out and she hugged the errant boy to her breast. Finally, she broke the silence of the night. "Noah? Why . . . why are you here?" Did she dare ask? Would he tell her what she wanted to hear?

He nibbled softly on her earlobe. "I thought you'd never ask. I came to make mad, passionate love to you, Wildcat. God! I've missed you! Do you know how lonely that damn cabin is without you?"

Charly giggled, feeling almost giddy and light-headed with the excitement of having Noah with her, so close. "I know how lonely the big city is without you! I thought you'd never come here—that I'd never see you again! I thought we'd never make mad, passionate love again! What are we waiting for?"

He nuzzled her ear and neck, his marvelous, velvety

beard tickling her, delighting her. "I'm waiting for you to stop crying. Either you're happy or you're sad. Make up your mind. If you're going to cry, I'll hold you. But if you're happy, we'll make love and make us both happy."

"No more crying, I promise. Couldn't you tell they were tears of happiness? I'm very happy to see you, Noah. I've missed you like you could never in a million years know! And I'm eager!" She kissed him fiercely on the lips, surprising him with her darting, teasing tongue.

Noah returned her passionate embrace, pulling her tightly against his unyielding, muscular body. She was soft, pliable, willing. He was hard, insatiable, demanding. They had been so long without each other, it was as if they were starved. And they indulged ravenously in the gratifying delicacy each offered. Their ecstasy was mutually shared as unspoken consent was agreed upon, and Noah swung her up in his powerful arms. At last! They were together at long last! Gently, he placed her on the bed.

Charly started to unbutton her wrinkled blouse, but his hands stopped her.

"Let me. It's been so long, Charly. I want to enjoy every part of you." His hands moved deliberately down the buttons, gloriously opening her blouse. Briefly, Charly was glad the room was so dark that he couldn't see the wrinkled condition of her blouse. Oh—what she had almost done tonight! Almost.

He deftly unsnapped the front opening of her bra and pushed it back so that her creamy white breasts fell naturally into his hands. Noah caressed them both, admiringly, lovingly. His tongue darted and teased the tips to firm hardness. Charly caught her breath as the sensuous feelings radiated throughout her entire body, reaching an ecstatic peak as she arched against the pressure of his hand.

"Oh, Charly, I want you . . ." His voice was husky and he struggled feverishly with his own clothes.

This time Charly grabbed his large warm hands. "No, you'll have to wait. Let me . . ." And she proceeded to unbutton his shirt. She ran her hands slowly down his chest, her fingernails digging through the soft mat of dark hair, tickling, scraping, loving, sharing the excitement of his masculine body.

With a shudder, he stood and began to loosen his belt and zipper. "Get them off, woman—I can't wait for you another minute!"

Obligingly, hurriedly, Charly scooted out of her remaining clothes, as anxious for Noah as he was for her. Suddenly, after weeks of wondering, of being apart, the longed-for time was nigh, and they welcomed the event joyously and with exuberance. The feverish pitch of their passion reached a rapid and glorious zenith, as they clung breathlessly to each other. Afterward they lay quietly together, their bodies saying what no words could.

Noah stroked her hair, urging an unruly lock away from her temple, where damp tendrils curled. His hand was cool and soothing now, as was his voice.

"I've missed you, little Wildcat. I didn't realize just how much until tonight, when I saw you, touched you. I thought it was my imagination. And I had forgotten what a real wildcat you are!"

"Noah." Her voice sounded very small in the quiet darkness.

"Hmmm?" His was a rumble that vibrated through her.

"Noah . . . I love you. I have been so miserable without you." Would she regret confessing her deepest feelings to him? No. It was obvious she loved him. She hoped, waited expectantly for his avowal of love for her. He kissed her, touched her as though he was filled with love—or was it just his strong passion?

"Well, I'm here now. So let's enjoy the next few days, Wildcat."

140

"Few days?" A feeling of dread began eroding the joy she felt at having him with her.

"Um-hum. I'm here for the weekend. I have business tomorrow, but after that I'm free."

"Every minute? Just for me?" She ran her finger around his lips.

"If you have time for me!"

"If—of course I do! I want you with me every minute!"

He didn't hide the exasperation in his voice. "Hell, you'll have to cancel your social calendar then. I waited five hours for you tonight! Dozed on your sofa . . . made friends with your cat . . . fixed myself a sandwich."

Charly moaned to herself, remembering how she had spent her evening—and how it had almost ended up. "I'm glad you met Mitts and made yourself at home. If I had only known you were coming—"

"It was a spur-of-the-moment deal. Business in Atlanta. I knew I had to see you."

"See me? And that's not all!" She giggled, running her hand over his chest.

His delighted laughter was a low rumble. "I can't look at you without touching, Wildcat. You do marvelous, uncontrollable things to me!"

She smiled against his neck while her fingers traced imaginary lines through the feathery-soft hair on his chest. "Ummm, I'm glad. It would be embarrassing for me to carry you to bed!"

He pinched her nipple. "And you probably could do it, too!"

She trailed a fingernail down the dark hairline of his belly and further. "You bet I could—if I made up my mind to it."

He grabbed the teasing, tantalizing finger. "Careful, Charly. You'll create a recurrence . . . ." He pressed her hand to his mouth, kissing her fingertips.

"Promise?" she teased, caressing the lips and beard she loved to touch.

"Charly . . . it's late. Very late. I have a meeting tomorrow and you have to go to work. We'll have all weekend to talk and catch up." His voice was muffled, low and relaxed.

"Catch up? Let's catch up now, Noah!" she challenged with a laugh. She leaned over him and kissed him long and hard, relishing the delicious taste of his lips.

The temptation was too much for Noah, and his hands claimed her again. They felt hot on her cool body as he artfully compelled her to new pleasures of ecstasy. With a low groan, he pulled her over him. Charly's delightful laughter filled the night as she experienced ultimate pleasures with the man she loved.

Finally, they slumped together exhausted, their craving satiated. But Charly was still unable to relinquish to sleep.

"Noah, did you say you've been waiting here, in my apartment, for five hours?"

"Um-hum."

"How did you get in?" It occurred to her that he didn't have a key.

"I convinced your landlady I was your brother. You're going to have to do something about the trusting souls around here. It's dangerous."

"Mrs. Kline?" Charly giggled. "She would die if she realized her mistake! And probably boot me out! Now I have to go around acting like you're my brother! I can't hang on you or kiss you or . . ."

His voice was relaxed and sleepy. "It's late, Charly . . ."

"Noah, how do you expect me to sleep when you're here with me at last? And I haven't seen you in two months . . ."

"Seven weeks and four days, to be exact. And agonizing

ones at that. But now I'm here and I don't intend to leave until you throw me out!"

"Promise you'll stay? You know I'll *never* throw you out, Noah! I want you here forever!"

"Until Monday—go to sleep."

"Noah—"

"Like this." He turned on his side and curved around her warm body. And Charly slept deeply for the first time in weeks, enfolded in the security and love of Noah's chest and arms and legs.

CHAPTER TEN

"Where's Charly?" boomed Lewis, red-faced and irritated as he banged the phone down again.

His secretary looked up knowingly. She was well accustomed to his temperamental moods and went bustling in to soothe him. She wasn't as concerned about him as about those around him. He had been in the office exactly forty-five minutes and had managed to yell at four of the pool secretaries, bringing one of them to tears and alienating Ben Morrison, his deputy assistant, who told him to "go to hell" before stalking out. Now he was screaming about Charly, for Pete's sake. Maybe Charly had something to do with bringing about all this uproar.

"T.G.I.F." she whispered to the records girl as she slipped into Lewis's office. "Mr. Daniel, Charly hasn't reported in today." She smiled a wide fake smile and set another cup of hot coffee on his desk. "Do you want me to get her on the phone at home? Is it urgent?" This off-on-Friday business had gotten to be a habit for Charly and everyone at the office was aware of it. And resentment ran high that she could continue to do it and keep her job.

"No. Ah, no, thank you, Ann. Sick again, eh?" He nodded and muttered again, "Thank you," his first and only kind words of the day. The secretary quietly left Lewis gazing out at the morning's sun reflecting on the glass of the tall Coastal States Building. He chuckled under his breath. He understood why Charly wasn't at work this particular Friday. Or so he thought.

The late-morning sun finally reached Charly's second-floor window and slipped between the thick poplar branches that shaded it. A shaft of light boldly crossed Charly's peacefully sleeping countenance. She stirred, turned over, and snuggled into the empty space beside her. She reached over to touch him, to make sure he was really there and not just a dream. But the bed was empty.

Her eyes flew open immediately and she sat up quickly, the covers falling from her bare breasts. What if—

"Have some coffee, Charly?" His voice made her smile even before she saw him puttering in the small kitchen.

He walked toward her, shirtless, handsome—real—and smiled as he handed her the blue coffee mug. "Good morning, beautiful," he murmured before kissing her. His gaze dropped to her exposed breasts and she reached for the blue-flowered sheet.

"Aw, don't be modest, Wildcat. I like the view," he laughed. "After last night . . ."

Her brown eyes glowed, and she sputtered arrogantly, "After last night, what?"

Noah sat on the edge of the bed and leaned over her, placing a hand on either side of her, kissing her again, this time long and sensual. "After last night, I never want to leave you, Charly. I don't know how I stayed away so long."

"Then don't. Don't leave me—ever," she answered simply, her eyes very sincere, but her heart knowing the truth. She touched his face, caressed his cheek and velvety beard. Oh, how she wished he would always be within her reach, her kiss. But she was afraid he would not. "Kiss me," she begged, longing for his reassuring touch.

The feathery-light kiss intensified to a flood tide of love's passion. Noah's lips crushed hers fiercely, his teeth

145

threatened to damage her tender skin. His hands savagely roamed her body, then pulled her to him. His dark beard covered her face, smothering her, and she gasped painfully as he pressed her tender breasts tightly against his bare chest. At her low cry, he immediately released his grasp. He lightly showered her face with kisses and his hands gently slid over her.

"Oh, God, Charly, I'm sorry. The last thing in the world I want to do is to hurt you. I just lost . . ." He kissed her eyelids and trailed to her mouth, where his lips lovingly caressed her.

Her hand curved around his neck and she dug into the hair curled there. "It's just been so long, Noah. I want you, too. I wish—"

"Don't—" He silenced her with another kiss. "Don't wish—just enjoy."

One hand removed the coffee mug Charly still clutched and unzipped his jeans while the other threw the blue-flowered sheet back, exposing her luscious curves to the angular morning sun.

"What a way to start the day," he teased as he slid onto the bed beside her.

"Hmmm." She nuzzled his neck. "Beats coffee every time . . ."

Their easy-laughing conversation ceased as lips opened for each other and hands sought to please. Soon their bodies melded together in an ecstatic crescendo of love and passion while the sun rose higher to bathe them in warmth. Leisurely, they descended to a lingering, glistening embrace, not wanting to let go, but knowing they must.

"Please, don't leave me, Noah," Charly whispered.

His voice was still hoarse with passion. "You know I can't make any promises—not yet, Charly. But we will have a good time together. That I can promise."

146

"I know," she admitted, feeling the immediate gulf between them, although they still lay entwined.

Finally, he shifted away from her simmering ardor and pulled his jeans over his slim hips. "How about that coffee now, Wildcat?"

"Want to try it again, huh?" She smiled, gratified knowing he found her magnetic. It gave her a feeling of a little power over him—at least, as long as she was with him.

"I'll stay an arm's length away this time," he laughed as he moved easily to the kitchen. His lithe motions reminded Charly of the stealthy pacing of a caged tiger.

She chuckled. "I think the wrong person has the name 'Wildcat.' It seems to me that it fits you much better."

He smiled as he approached her again, a steamy mug in each hand. "Maybe you're right, Charly. But those first two days I knew you, you were like a wildcat—rebelling, scratching, fighting everything I said or did. After that, however, you tamed down to a cuddly kitten."

She took the mug and grinned good-naturedly with his teasing. "I just needed someone to cuddle with me!"

"So did I." His eyes still twinkled, but there was a seriousness to his tone. Then, adroitly, he changed the subject. "Don't you have to go to work sometime today? It's after ten."

Charly sipped leisurely from her mug and smiled smugly at him. "I'll call in sick in a few minutes. I don't want to miss a second with you." She didn't tell him that this off-on-miserable-Friday business was common for her. Only this time it was a marvelous Friday to be spent with Noah.

As if he read her mind, he answered, "I have a meeting today, Charly. I can't spend the entire day with you. I have some business to attend to, you know. Business lunch at noon."

She shrugged. "That's okay. As long as you spend the night." She grinned.

"Oh, yes! I wouldn't miss the night for anything!" He winked and Charly thrilled to his delightful teasing. He snapped his fingers as his memory was jogged. "That reminds me, Charly. I have reservations to stay tonight at the Peachtree Plaza Hotel. Would you like to spend the night there? It's very beautiful."

Charly raised her eyebrows. "Is that the one with the half-acre lake in the lobby? Wonder if they'd let me wade?"

"Not if I tell them your wading sometimes leads to skinny-dipping! Well, how about it? They have a pool and, of course, the lake. It's one of the most beautiful hotels you'll find anywhere."

She shook her thick mane. "I'm not hunting hotels." *I'm trying to hang on to my man.* "Would you mind terribly if we don't go public, Noah? I think I want you right here with me." There was something possessive about having him in her own bed, and she didn't want to let go.

He shrugged. "It's fine with me. But I insist on taking you out tonight. I already have reservations at Nikolai's Roof for nine. It's a marvelous restaurant and I want you to enjoy it. Also, I want to show you off a little. That is, if I'm not interrupting any of your weekend plans by arriving so unexpectedly."

"I have no plans this weekend except to be with you, Noah." Should she tell him about last night with Lewis? Her desperation? Her agony over the last two months? No—didn't he say to enjoy the present? "Nikolai's Roof? I've heard of it, but—how did you get reservations? They're booked weeks in advance for the weekends."

"Connections, my dear Charly. Connections!" He reached for something on her coffee table. "Here, I brought you a little something from the mountain country. Thought it might remind you of the halcyon days spent at Noah's ark!" He laughed as he casually tossed a small box in her lap.

Charly sat up delightedly, trying to cover herself with the sheet. "A gift? Great! And it's not even my birthday!" She set aside her coffee mug and tore at the calico ribbon that adorned the simple box. Inside, nestled in blue tissue paper, was an exquisite wood carving of a small wild rabbit. As she lifted it carefully out of the box, she could see the precise detail of the carving, right down to the tiny whiskers. It was quite unique.

"Ooooh, Noah," she breathed. "It's just gorgeous . . ." For a moment she was speechless and gazed at the miniature rabbit through misty eyes. "It's so . . . fine. Thank you, Noah. It does remind me of our days in the mountains together. Remember the little rabbit you tried to sketch on that last morning—" Her voice caught and there was a moment of strained silence between them. They both recalled—all too well.

Noah boldly launched through the heavy reticence. "I'm glad you like him, Charly. He was made by an old man who has carved miniatures for fun and relaxation all his life. Now he's making a good living by selling them. And he's preserving his craft by teaching at the local college. I was very impressed by his work and thought you would be, too."

"Oh, I am! And I'm so glad you brought it to me in person." Her voice dwindled as Noah kissed her lips and nose, then offered to make breakfast.

" 'Never disturb a man who likes to cook' is my motto," Charly laughed, ecstatic to have him near. She wanted to savor every moment with him. She enjoyed just watching him prowl around her small studio apartment as if he belonged there.

"I'm going to find a special place of honor for this little fellow," she pledged determinedly, throwing back the sheet and slipping across the room.

Mitts, the cat, jumped to the back of the sofa, alarmed at the sudden activity of his mistress.

"There. How's that?" She stepped back to assess the little rabbit's position on the glass étagère.

"Perfect! Just terrific!" agreed Noah, openly admiring the spectacle of Charly fluttering around the room nude.

"He does look perfect right there between the violets." She smiled with satisfaction.

"I think he'd be happier between the roses!"

"There aren't any roses—" The amused look on his face told her he was teasing her again. She threw a sofa pillow at him. "Back to your pans, chef!"

He dodged the pillow easily and laughed aloud as he went about his task. "How does a mushroom omelet and biscuits sound?"

"Biscuits?"

"Sure." He padded barefooted and bare-chested around the kitchen, reminding Charly again of the casual, carefree days in the cabin. "Biscuits are my specialty."

"No they aren't! Your talents aren't confined to the kitchen!" She grinned devilishly, knowing she had gotten him back.

"Huh?" He was hunting for pans, making a loud rattling noise as he rustled through her collection.

She gave him a disgusted look, then shrugged. The timing for the joke had passed. Oh, well, there would be other times. "Biscuits sound great, Noah. Fattening, but great. I don't think I've had a biscuit since I left the mountain cabin."

He gazed at her slim, bare body. "Looks as though you haven't had enough of anything to eat, Charly. Have you lost weight?"

How could he be that observant? She swung her long hair defensively and it fell loosely over her shoulders. "I've been busy." She disappeared into the bathroom. How could she tell him of the miserable days—and nights—she

150

sat waiting to hear from him, hoping, crying alone in the night?

By the time she emerged from her shower, Noah was setting the table. She wore a short satiny robe that scarcely hid her bare curves. He had donned a light blue shirt, leaving the shirttail casually hanging loose. Oh, she had forgotten how good he looked in blue, his dark hair dominant and those blue eyes outstanding. This was the man she had tried to forget? Thank God, it was impossible. He filled her mind as well as her imagination.

Slowly, she walked to him and wrapped her arms around his waist, lightly scratching his back with her fingernails, then pressing him tightly to her. Oh, he felt good against her!

Noah's arms enfolded her, and he kissed the top of her head. She leaned against his chest, listening to the heavy beat of his heart as it pulsed regularly through her.

He held her that way for a long time, and Charly felt marvelous in his arms. She wanted it to last forever.

"God, I've missed you, Charly." His voice rumbled in her ear.

"I've missed you, too, Noah." She turned her face to him, seeking the sweet assurance of his lips. His kiss told her what he refused to say, and she clung to that feeling—that hope.

They parted at last and Noah reached for a plain brown sack on the counter. "I brought some gifts from Walt. I think he likes you, Charly. When I told him I'd be seeing you, he insisted that I take these to you."

Noah lifted a quart jar filled with golden honey surrounding a long section of the honeycomb.

"Great! Look! It's beautiful!" She smiled her pleasure and noted that it would take her forever to eat a quart of honey.

"And . . ." He raised another jar—a gallon at least. "Blackberry wine!"

Charly clapped her hands with delight. "Marvelous! Oh, I've missed it. What a lovely color!" She admired the clear burgundy hue of the wine. "You'll have to help me drink this, Noah. I'll never be able to finish it. Nor the honey. It's just too much."

"My pleasure," he said, smiling.

"How generous of Walt to send them."

"Yes, considering . . ." His digging comment was left unsaid as he buttered a delectable biscuit.

They ate finally, exchanging small talk about what they had been doing in the past weeks.

"How's the job?" Nothing was mentioned about the lifetime-lease project that had propelled Charly into his mountain life.

"Oh, fine." She didn't say that she hated it more every day—her precious, valuable job and the continued problems of working with Lewis Daniel. Now, after the episode last night, it would be even worse. "How's Walt?" She smiled at the thought of the gentle old man.

"He's fine. Ornery as ever."

"How did you pry yourself away from the mountain?" Was there a sarcastic edge to her question?

But he smiled good-naturedly. "I gravitate to the civilized world every few weeks to check on the business. This opportunity came up, and it was advisable that I take advantage of it. I don't usually travel, but the fact that you are in Atlanta made the decision to come here much easier."

"But if it weren't for business, you wouldn't have come." Charly couldn't help her acid tone.

"If it weren't for you being here, I would have sent someone else to take care of this," he snapped. "Look, Charly, I don't want to argue with you. I'll be here such a short time, let's not spend our time snipping at each other."

Charly bit her lip, already regretting her sharp tongue,

152

but unable to control her bitterness that it had taken him so long to come to her. Maybe she was the wildcat after all. "You're right, Noah. I don't want to argue either. I guess I've still got some of the wildcat in me."

"Oh, but I like you that way, Wildcat." He rose to take his dishes to the sink and kissed the tip of her nose on the way.

Like? *Like?* Charly almost broke into tears at his choice of words. But she managed to say casually, "Just leave the dishes, Noah. I'll have time to clean up while you're away."

He readily agreed. "Sounds like a good idea, especially since I cooked the breakfast. Taking turns with this kitchen stuff is only fair, you know. Anyway, I need to shower and change. I have a meeting in an hour."

She motioned toward the small bathroom. "Please feel free to use my *indoor* facilities. The toilet flushes and we even have *hot* and cold running water!"

"My, my! Such modern conveniences here in the big city!"

Charly curled contentedly on the bed. She was totally in heaven with a mug of coffee to sip, watching the man she loved. In less than an hour Noah transformed from the casual, rugged, mountain man Charly knew so well to a distinguished, well-dressed businessman in a three-piece suit who was a stranger to her. She couldn't believe how incredibly handsome he looked as he shrugged into the gray pinstripe suit coat that completed his attire. Yet, with his dark beard, he retained a look apart, a rather mysterious appearance.

It occurred to Charly that Noah was an enigma to her, too. She knew him as one man—rough, natural, sensitive. And yet he stood before her as someone totally different— tough, capable, all business. Which was he—really? She accepted his perfunctory kiss, knowing he was already preoccupied with his upcoming meeting. She stood at the window and watched wistfully as Noah climbed into the rented Caprice. He had the look of a wealthy man who ran his ages-old family business with an iron hand. Was this the man with whom she had fallen in love?

By four he was back, twirling her around the apartment, teasing her, making love to her with such rich abandon that she wondered if she had really seen him as the staid businessman she had earlier imagined. Oh, God! How she loved him!

Later they showered together and Noah helped her wash her hair.

"Ummm, that feels wonderful," she said, purring, as they stood glistening wet and Noah towel-dried her thick mane vigorously. "You're spoiling me, y'know."

"And don't you forget it," he answered, and wrapped the towel around her head before grabbing a large bath towel for himself. He left her in the bathroom and she could hear him rummaging through his luggage.

"How are you wearing your hair tonight, Wildcat?"

She struggled with the brush and blow drier, trying to twist the ends in just the right casual curl. "I thought I'd wear it down. Why? Does it matter to you?"

"Oh, no." His answer was casual enough. "Just wondering."

Finally, Charly achieved the look she wanted and applied just enough makeup to enhance her large brown eyes and rosy lips. She opened the closet door and studied her limited wardrobe.

Noah's voice had a tinge of humor as he advised her. "Wear something feminine tonight, Wildcat. I want to see what you look like in something besides jeans—and *my* jeans, at that!"

Charly sighed dubiously. There wasn't much choice. "Now, where did you say we were going?"

"I'm taking you to the zenith, the top of the town

154

tonight, Wildcat. First, drinks at the Hyatt's Polaris. Then at Nikolai's Roof, atop the Hilton."

"Sounds terrific, Noah. They say the view's beautiful up there." She selected an off-white, creamy satin gown, long, with a dramatic slit on one side, tied on one shoulder. As she adjusted it, she glanced into the full-length mirror. The dress hung loosely over her curves and clung seductively around her breasts.

"Well, the view's certainly going to be gorgeous tonight," Noah acknowledged, admiring the lovely woman before him.

"How do you like it?" She twirled, the side slit showing one long, alluring leg.

"Yes, I'd say you've made the full transition from mountain girl to lovely lady! You look gorgeous, Wildcat." His eyes traveled over her enticing figure and bare shoulder.

"Speaking of changes, you don't look like the same mountaineer I met in Simm's Hollow."

Charly let her eyes roam his masculine frame from his gray coat and vest to his gray lightweight wool slacks that stretched over his sinewy hips and legs. "You don't look like you came from a mountain, sir." She pulled teasingly on his beard until he lowered his face to kiss her.

"Same man, Charly," he murmured as he ran one hand luxuriously under her mass of hair and pulled her close. He kissed her hard and she melted against him. But before she could gather into his arms, he pushed her away and turned her sideways.

His hand was still around her neck and he instructed, "Hold your hair up, Charly."

She obeyed him and lifted her hair before she realized what he was doing.

"There . . ." he said with satisfaction. He turned her around to face him, a powerful hand on each shoulder. His

155

eyes registered a special glow as he assessed her from head to foot. "Ah, perfect—you're beautiful, Charly."

Anxiously, she sought the mirror. When her reflection focused clearly, she gasped at her own image. The necklace that Noah had attached to her slender neck held a magnificent cluster of diamonds that nestled in the hollow of her throat—three circular-cut diamonds arched above a pear-shaped stone. The splendid display was elegantly suspended and presented a glittering emphasis to the swell of her breasts. The diamonds shimmered with an inner glow of blue-white, giving a complete, harmonious splendor to her dazzling appearance. Charly could only stare, her round eyes traveling from the diamonds to her own shocked countenance and back to the glimmering stones. She touched them gingerly to make sure it wasn't her imagination.

"Oooh, Noah . . ."

"How do you like it, Charly?" he prompted.

"I . . . I love it . . ." But it occurred to her that she couldn't possibly accept such an expensive gift from Noah. Her brown eyes sought his. "Noah, I . . . I can't accept this—it's just too . . . too much." She couldn't imagine the monetary value of such a gorgeous display of diamonds. Several thousand, at least. And Noah gave them to her as a gift? She shook her head in dazed amazement and looked back to her image.

Noah stood behind her, his hands resting on her shoulders near the diamonds. Two fingers caressed her slightly and his eyes were serious and somewhat smoky. "Yes you can, Charly. I want you to have them. And they look gorgeous on you—better than my wildest dream." His voice was low and quieting—persuasive. She'd heard that tone before.

Charly shook her head again. "Noah, I can't—I just—"

He interrupted her. "Charly, listen to me." He turned her around to face him, his hands lightly on her neck, tormenting her with his touch. "We are no longer children. We are adults, with adult desires. One of my desires is to give you this small gift. Please accept it." His voice was barely above a whisper. "Charly, I have never given you anything. And you have given me so much happiness. Diamonds are forever—and that's how I want it to be with us."

His mouth claimed hers then, and Charly knew that she would accept Noah's gift—and whatever he wanted for their life together.

CHAPTER ELEVEN

Their first stop was atop the Hyatt Regency for drinks. They glided through the atrium lobby, two people in love with only eyes for each other. Charly was a vision with her chestnut hair framing her beaming face, the diamond necklace flashing prominently above the swell of her breasts, her satin gown flowing seductively, while every step revealed the length of one shapely leg. She had never been so happy and it was obvious in her face.

Noah was tall, handsome, and enigmatic with his ebony beard and shock of collar-length hair. He seemed to hover protectively around his lady, clearly proud to be her escort. Yet the way his eyes caressed her revealed he was more than her escort. Much more.

Charly hid her face against Noah's sheltering shoulder as they zoomed twenty-two stories in the glass-bubble elevator high above the electric city of Atlanta to the revolving restaurant. The view was magnificent and Charly excitedly pointed out the Omni International complex, the Coastal States Building, Underground Atlanta made up of shops and nightclubs, the Peachtree Center Plaza Hotel, her own office . . . But the view was secondary. They savored every moment together, their eyes revealing the love they shared. People viewed them discreetly, thinking they were a honeymoon couple, breaking away from their privacy for such basic necessities as food and drink. And they were—almost.

They briefly toured the Omni, watching ice skaters swirl on the glassy surface, and ended up at Nikolai's Roof for dinner. They sipped a light French Chablis and tasted delectable mushrooms stuffed with crab, spinach, and cheese. The pheasant was rich and savory and included a pungent hunter's sauce thick with mushrooms and wine. They lingered over coffee and cheesecake, each trying to prolong the enjoyment of the evening to the fullest.

Noah toyed with his coffee cup, running his finger along the edge impatiently. "I have to work again tomorrow, Charly." He could see the disappointment in her eyes even in the dim candlelight.

"On Saturday?"

He nodded. "Something came up and we have to continue tomorrow."

She tried to be gracious. "Aw, shucks. I was planning to take you shopping, tour the Underground, and wear you out climbing Stone Mountain." She smiled, but the disappointment was there.

"Sorry. My day starts early. I have to pick my lawyer up at the airport, then we have a meeting until . . ." He shrugged.

"How long?" Suddenly it was important to know how much time she would have with him.

"It depends. There are some details to be worked out, but a merger is in the works. I'm buying out a company here in Atlanta. They will serve as the Georgia distributor for our plant. Eventually I'd like to see them become the Southern distributor. Location is good, plant facilities—management needs beefing up, but we can handle that."

"Noah, does that mean you will be coming to Atlanta more often?" Her voice rose with expectancy.

He smiled tightly. "It might. There'll be work to do here."

Her smile improved and the disappointment in her eyes dissolved. "Great! I like the idea more every minute. I

159

guess I can spare you a few hours tomorrow. So long as you promise to come back."

His dark hand covered hers. "Of course I will."

Why did she doubt it, even when he looked her in the eyes and said it? She hated herself for doubting him. His blue eyes were sincere tonight. They told her he cared for her—loved her. She could believe his eyes, couldn't she? He had given her the diamonds as symbols of everlasting love. His love. She touched them tenderly—tangible proof of his love even if he refused to say it.

"Let's go home, Charly." His voice was low and urgent. "I've had enough of being public tonight." There was a special glow in his passionate blue eyes that urged her, tantalized her, assured her.

Charly rose and nodded in agreement. Her brown eyes smiled their consent, knowing his desires even before he whispered in her ear as he assisted her with the chair, "I want to rush you home and strip that beautiful gown off your luscious body and take you right there on the floor."

Charly's bronze eyes widened with amazed delight as Noah's provocative language sent goose bumps down her legs. She looked around quickly to see if they had eavesdroppers, then to her handsome escort for the evening. He smiled at her pleasantly, serenely, and murmured quietly, "Just walk out normally and pretend you don't notice the bulge in my pants."

Charly's mouth opened into a small O, as if she couldn't believe Noah was tantalizing her with his words. She didn't *dare* look down at him! She obeyed the pressure of his hand on her back and cut her eyes around to steal a glance at him. The devil! Noah's countenance remained placid as he nodded graciously to the waiter and escorted her from Nikolai's Roof, his arm politely around her waist. The handsome young couple, obviously honeymooners, glided from the public's view, two people in love with eyes only for each other.

* * *

The instant that her apartment door locked them from the intrusion of the outside world, his hands were claiming his treasure, seeking to fulfill his publicly whispered promise.

"Oh, God, Charly. This evening has been pure torture!" One hand cupped her satin-covered breast, while the other slipped under her dark halo of hair and gently pulled her to him.

"Noah, it's been a beautiful evening! I've loved it. Eating high above Atlanta was a special pleasure for me. And everything was marvelous! Your gift—the diamonds—and being with you made me feel like a queen tonight, Noah." Her eyes were dark and provocative, her voice almost a whisper, as Noah's hand continued to hold his prize and his thumb pressed sensitive, soft places. A sharp intake of her breath let him know she was feeling the same sensuous pleasures he felt.

"You were a queen tonight. Didn't you see the heads turn when you walked by? I was jealous as hell." His thumb circled the rosy tip, bringing it to a quick, sharp focus. "You were the most beautiful part of the evening, Wildcat. And that made it torture for me. I couldn't touch you . . ." His entire hand mastered her smooth, silken breast, enjoying the slick feel of the material over her bare flesh. "And I couldn't kiss you . . ." He kissed her lips softly, quickly, tantalizing her lips as his hand continued its pleasurable roaming over her silk-covered body.

"Oooh." A small moan escaped Charly's burning lips.

Her arms climbed the wall of his chest, then slowly her fingers trailed around his neck until they buried themselves in his thick hair. His mouth sought hers again, this time in a fierce encounter that opened her lips to his forceful, probing tongue. She felt powerless against him and met his advances tentatively, cautiously offering her tongue as well as her body. He responded with a shudder

161

to the touch of her tongue against his and slid his hands around to her back, pressing ever stronger.

His power intensified as his arms molded her firmly to his steel-hard frame, crushing her rising breasts to his muscular chest. His hands reached behind her buttocks, lifting until her pelvis fit solidly against his and she could feel his maleness against her.

"Noah . . . oh, Noah," she muttered, leaning weakly against him.

Just when she thought he would engulf her completely, somehow pressing her into him, he abruptly released the painful pressure of her flesh into his. He allowed her tongue to trail the shape of his mouth, tantalizing him, plundering his mouth the way he had hers. She enjoyed being the aggressor.

He lowered her feet to the floor and, with his hands on her rib cage, pushed her from him. His eyes raked over her savagely, and his hands rose to grasp both breasts, almost roughly, then traveled on to her slender neck. She shuddered weakly with the passion his touch aroused in her and swayed slightly, since he no longer supported her.

"Lean back. The wall will brace you, Charly." His voice was thick with passion as his hands roamed under her hair and around her shoulders.

Charly lifted her face to his for another kiss—wet, probing, fierce. She found that she had to obey and lean against the wall for support from his piercing kiss. As her passion heightened, she felt his leg separate hers, his knee applying pressure against her. A low guttural sound escaped her throat, and she knew she couldn't stand much longer, even with a wall behind her for support.

Although his knee remained firmly in its wedge against her, Noah moved back to admire her. His fingers quickly released the shoulder clasp and the dress slowly slid down her body, revealing her full, creamy breasts with their taut nipples, her flat belly. It gathered in a rumpled heap around her hips where his knee stopped the continued descent of the material. When he finally moved, the dress slid rapidly to the floor, a creamy-white circle around Charly's feet.

"Get those hose off." The raspy command was actually Noah's voice.

By the time Charly fumbled to remove the offending panty hose, Noah had shucked his jacket and shirt. He stood bare-chested before her, glistening muscles emphasized by a balanced scattering of dark masculine hair.

Charly looked up into his eyes—dark, passion-filled, showing no reflection of her own bare body trembling before him. She stood motionless, boldly enduring his all-encompassing gaze. She was proud of her body and the assurance that she could please him. This was a brief halt in their lovemaking, a moment when she could revel in the knowledge that ecstasy would soon come for both of them. She said it with her eyes. *I love you, Noah.*

"My God, Charly, what a vision—you're beautiful," he murmured, his hands no longer able to refrain from touching her fiery skin. One hand rested possessively on one of her hips, while the other stimulated her senses to wild intoxication. A single finger trailed leisurely from her parted lips to the hollow of her throat, where the diamonds still nestled as a single adornment of his love. His finger burned the roundness of first one breast, then the other, stopping long enough to punctuate the hard buttons at the tips. The tantalizing finger continued its flaming trail over her feminine hip, then around to the tender, sensitive inner thigh, where an excruciating passion blazed her limbs. She shuddered against him as he continued his trail of sublime arousal.

Her fingers fumbled clumsily with his trousers, the stiff belt, the stubborn zipper. "Hurry, Noah!"

Finally, with one hand, he helped her strip off his clothes, never halting his gentle probing of her willing body. He lifted her buttocks again, fitting her pelvis perfectly against his. This time there were no clothes to prevent their ultimate pleasure. Their bodies locked together in love, and Charly clung to Noah's shoulders as he gently lowered her to the floor.

He kept his word, given so brazenly in the restaurant, and took her before they crossed the small room to the bed. But Charly was glad. She didn't think she would have made it to the bed. Finally, Noah carried her to the comfort of her bed, but it wasn't necessary. They only wanted to be together and slept peacefully in each other's arms. Charly was in paradise, encircled in Noah's arms, graced with the diamonds of their forever love.

The next morning, by the time Charly was awake, Noah was already gone to take care of his infernal business. He left the coffee on WARM and a brief note on the table: GET BACK IN BED, WILDCAT! I WANT YOU THERE WHEN I RETURN! N.

She smiled at his lusty, witty note and looked around the quiet, empty apartment. Her eyes fell on the white dress she had worn the night before. It lay in the same circle where it had dropped from her body. She shuddered with delight just remembering the events that had led up to and followed the discarding of the dress. She rubbed her arms vigorously as chill bumps ran their length. She remembered his electric touch, his slow appreciation of her, his power. Why did he have to leave so soon? She wasn't prepared to awake alone. She didn't want to give him up yet. But would she ever—*ever*—be ready for him to leave? Probably not. No, definitely not!

She felt something tug at her neck and automatically reached to caress the elegant diamond necklace that still encircled her. The stones were cold and hard to her touch, a reminder that they would always be there—forever. But would Noah's love? She walked to the mirror and gazed at the image she saw there: a simple, tousle-haired brunette with a slim, high-breasted body adorned like a queen with diamonds. She fingered them again. If he doesn't love me, why did he give me these? she wondered. Why does he look at me that special way? Why . . . last night? Yes, oh yes! That was an act of love! For me it was! She turned away, afraid to think any further.

When he returned, Charly wasn't in bed as he had instructed. She had been busy cleaning the apartment, picking up discarded clothes, making the bed. Everything appeared neat once again, the way she liked it. She was dressed in casual slacks and a sweater, appeared happily in his arms, ready to take him out and show him Atlanta.

He wrapped his arm around her, leading her across the room. "But, Charly, I thought I left the message clear. I want you there!" With a fast motion, he reached under her legs and lifted her high before swinging her onto the bed in an ungracious heap.

"Damn you!" she squealed. "I can read! But I want to take you to Stone Mountain today. You should be homesick for mountains by now, so I thought I'd let you see our nearest competition to the Smokies!"

He shook his head and kissed her soundly. "I'm only homesick for you, Wildcat. I never get enough!" He began working on her sweater, his hands under it, fingers pressing her soft, braless breasts.

"Noah! No-ah!" she giggled. His hands never stopped.

"Yes—come on, Wildcat! I'll beat you getting undressed!" He bounded off the bed and began stripping.

Charly sat up and folded her arms. "Noah—are you serious? You're crazy, you know! Aren't you going to tell me about your meeting? How did it go? You know, all the important stuff like did you buy that company?"

Noah stood before her, completely nude and waiting. "I'm serious. Come here, Wildcat . . ."

Charly squealed and tried to get away from his grasping

hands. Of course, she couldn't. As he pinned her to the bed and covered her face with kisses, she gasped, "Aren't you going to tell . . . me . . . about your . . . meeting?"

"Not now, woman. I'm busy concentrating on important things. Small talk will come later . . . "

Charly was adamant about taking Noah outdoors in the Atlanta countryside. And Noah obviously wanted to shower Charly with his complete attention. So they compromised. Noah got his way. And afterward he helped her remake the bed. They managed to spend part of the afternoon at Stone Mountain. So Charly was the winner after all! How could she lose when Noah was with her! Delighted, ecstatic, content—her emotional level was at its peak.

They hiked the trails and rode the cablecar and sipped Cokes while admiring the immense Civil War sculptures carved in the huge wall of stone.

"Imagine doing that for a living! How long did it take? What a fantastic job!" Noah was obviously impressed. "So precise, so detailed!"

But Charly had seen the carvings before. She giggled. "What if you were the world's greatest stone sculptor and afraid of heights!"

He narrowed his eyes and viewed it prospectively. "Hmmm, you could always do it blindfolded! Of course, someone like you, who can't even travel in the glass elevator at the Hyatt without hiding your eyes, would be in big trouble! The world's greatest stone sculptor would have to find another occupation."

"Any suggestions?" She tucked her arm into his and snuggled against his firm, warm shoulder.

"Sure." He bent his head close to hers. "You could be the world's greatest lover—and I'd hire you. Now I expect my employees to be loyal—no others could seek your services, of course!"

"Agreed! I think I'm hired!" She smiled happily, tugging on his marvelous beard. "I like your mountain better anyway, Noah. It's more . . . private."

"*My* mountain? My God, Charly! That mountain belongs to the whole country! That's what you were fighting for, remember?"

The tone between them changed immediately.

She looked away, remembering. "Yeah, I know. Well, the battle plan's changed."

"But not the ultimate goal." His voice was hard, knowing, prophetic.

"Maybe. Lewis hasn't mentioned it lately. I hope it's been put to rest." A dread pervaded her being, for she knew the case hadn't been entirely closed.

"So do I." But he, too, knew they hadn't heard the last of the lifetime-lease affair.

After spending yet another amorous night with Noah, Charly was so totally immersed in her love of the elusive man that she became depressed at the mere thought that he would be leaving soon. She was living with him—again—and loving it. Again. They spent Sunday morning just being together. Later she couldn't even remember what they had done. She figured they ate, but didn't know what. She recalled walking among some trees with him, arm in arm. She assumed it was in the nearby park, but she wasn't sure.

What she remembered, all too well, was their final conversation. Later she regretted her words. She hated what she had said, but knew her reasoning was right. It had to be. It had cost her a tremendous personal loss. Perhaps if she hadn't pressed . . .

"Where are you going when you leave here, Noah?" Her voice was tight, for saying it finally made it real.

He walked to the window. "Back to the cabin. I need to check on Walt."

"When will I see you again?" She hated talking to his

back and wished he would turn around so she could see his eyes.

"I don't know. I'll try to get back to Atlanta . . . soon. Since we've purchased the other company, someone will need to make the transition smooth."

"Will that be you?" Her voice was expectant.

His broad shoulders shrugged. "Don't know, Charly. I don't usually do that sort of thing . . ."

"Why not? It would give you reason to be here." Her voice betrayed her anxiety.

But his was low and steady. "I . . . don't need a business reason, Charly. You're enough. I'll come back . . . to you."

"Noah, let me go back with you. I . . . I can't stand the thought of being without you again . . . for God knows how long. Take me with you." She couldn't believe her own pleading voice.

He turned around then, and she could see the pained, almost panicked expression in his azure eyes. "No! You know you can't do that, Charly! I can't . . ."

"Why not? I just want to be with you."

He spread his hands. "It's impossible. Now is not the time."

"Noah, I . . . I love you. Will there ever be a 'time'?"

He ran his hand through his hair abstractly. "I . . . I don't know, Charly. Things are too complicated now—too confused."

"Maybe you're confused, but I'm not! What are you talking about anyway? Love?" She was on her feet now, facing him adamantly. Damn him! What did he think he was doing to her?

"No. I . . . I don't think I'm ready—" He placed his hands on her arms. "Just don't press me, Charly. I'm not ready for the emotional obligation of you . . . or anyone else. I may never be. I don't want it, don't you understand?"

Charly's voice was shrill as she reached near hysteria.

"Oh, yes, I'm beginning to understand, all right! You just want to have a bed to come to occasionally! And the expensive gift was to make sure I'd keep it warm for you!"

He shook her slightly, tightening his grip. "No, Charly, that's not true! I . . . meant what I said about . . . everything . . ."

"Then why did you come here?"

He searched her angry face with obscure, confused eyes, then turned away from her. "I don't know. I just had to see you."

"*See* me?" she railed. "Then why didn't you just rent a car and sit on the street until I came down. Then you could have seen me! Why bother to come in? Why did you have to . . . touch me?" She was near tears.

"I don't know . . ." His voice was low and empty.

"What did you think this weekend would do for *me*? Or did you think of that? Did you want to build me up again, so I could fall flat on my face when you walk out the door? Then I could sit over here waiting and hoping and wishing you would have another business crisis so you would have to fly back over here to Atlanta to 'see' me? Well, I can't stand the uncertainty! I don't want to be built up only to be dropped at the end of the weekend! I can't live like this! I won't be your mistress. I must know—"

"Charly . . . Charly, please—" Hesitantly, he took a step toward her.

But she backed away, her voice harsh. "Don't touch me! If you don't love me, just get the hell out of my apartment —and my *life!*" She trembled with the emotion and shock of what she had just said to Noah. Her love . . .

His face contorted with inner pain. It was as if she had just slapped him and he didn't protest what she said. He looked hurt and knew he was defeated—they were defeated. Yet he did not seek a reprieve.

"I'm sorry, Charly. The last thing in the world I want to do is to hurt you. But it looks like that's just what I've

169

done." And with those words he walked out of her apartment—and out of her life.

Well—it's what she wanted, wasn't it? She told him to make the choice! Demanded that he tell her now! "Oh, how I hate you, Noah Van Horn!" she shouted at the closed door, and in an angry rage she jerked the gold and diamond necklace from her neck and flung it against the wall. "And take your expensive diamonds, too! I don't want them!"

But he did not take them. He left the diamonds with Charly—the solid symbol of their forever love. And the necklace lay on the floor of her apartment, near where her satiny dress had been dropped in a circle at Charly's feet—near where Noah had made love to her. The golden latch was pulled out of shape so that it didn't clasp properly anymore, but the arch of diamonds over the beautiful pear-shaped stone were still intact. *Diamonds are forever.*

CHAPTER TWELVE

"Come on in, Charly. So glad you could make it today." Lewis's voice was edged with sarcasm.

He had been malicious since the night Charly had refused his physical advances. He had never forgiven her that injustice and wouldn't discuss it with her. Charly had even tried to patch it up and offered weak apologies, but working conditions had deteriorated badly. They clashed often and over everything. They just couldn't agree on simple goals, much less on complicated strategy, so she tried to avoid confrontations with him. But this time was different. The lifetime lease in the Smokies had been revived and Charly was requested, in Lewis's domineering way, to sit in on the strategy session. Actually, she wanted to be a part of it. She wanted to know what he was planning. So she struggled to make it to work on her "miserable Friday" in spite of her own strong desire to call in sick.

There were other things to do on Fridays to help her forget—but none of them ever worked. Noah was still on her mind—especially this morning as she slid into a chair opposite Ben Morrison. Lewis paced the floor near the small conference table, his mannerisms asserting his dominant position with those in the room.

"It seems that this Van Horn fellow has been living, full time, at Simms's cabin for two and a half years!" Lewis's mention of Noah's name snapped Charly immediately to the events of the meeting. What was he saying about Noah?

Ben was reading a dossier and making notes on the side. "What is he doing up there?"

"Good question. He runs a furniture manufacturing plant out of Charlotte—" Lewis was interrupted.

"Now?" Ben was trying to be thorough.

"Let me finish, Ben. Now he owns a family business, this furniture company, and uses the mountain cabin as his refuge. About two—"

This time it was Charly who interrupted. "That's not true! He doesn't use the cabin as his 'refuge.' He takes care of Walt—"

"Is that so? Well, Charly, maybe you'd like to tell us more. If you'd been willing to do your job months ago, you could have informed us all about this Noah Van Horn and saved time and the money expended to have this damn investigation!" Lewis's eyes gleamed viciously at her.

"You're so tactful, Lewis. I can tell this is going to be a pleasure."

"Goddamn, Charly! I sent you up there six months ago to do a simple job. You ended up staying two weeks and came back unwilling to complete the case! Not only that— you refuse to give up information you have about the subjects. Now what the hell am I supposed to do—pat you on the back?"

"The 'subjects'?" Charly flamed at his terminology.

"Come on, Charly. What's Van Horn doing up there? Running booze?"

"No! Of course not!"

"Is there any being run? Maybe Walt—" Lewis was persistent.

"No!"

"What, then? Is he using the place as a hunting lodge?"

Charly could feel the anger rising in her and she knew

172

she had to keep cool. "No! He's just . . . just staying with his friend, I guess."

Lewis dismissed her comment with a shrug of his hand. "Well, Van Horn doesn't bother me that much. He appeared about two years ago after the death of his wife and kid in a car wreck. But he's violating the law just by being there. So he'll be easy enough to dispose of. A court order will take care of him. It's the old man we have to contend with."

Charly lifted her head defiantly. What was Lewis leading up to?

After a pause, he continued, slowly setting up his plan. "Now, Charly, I wanted you to sit in on this session to see if you could shed any light on the situation. Or if you would help somehow. You lived with Simms for nearly two weeks. What is he like? Pretty senile, huh?"

"Senile? Of course not! He's perfectly normal—alert, active . . . witty . . ." A smile spread across her face as she remembered the old man. "And he plays a harmonica—"

"My God, Charly! The old guy's eighty-nine! He can't be alert as all that! You said that Van Horn took care of him. He must need supervision."

"No, he doesn't need supervision. Lewis, what are you getting at?"

He sighed heavily and cast a disgusted look at Ben that clearly said, "This is not going to be as easy as we thought." He cleared his throat. "Charly, you won't have to do another thing with this case. Ben, here, is taking it over for you. You won't have to go back there and face those people. We are going to proceed with the strategy already discussed, months ago, before your . . . uh, excursion. You remember that plan, don't you?" He paused dramatically and looked at her. When she didn't answer, he continued, undaunted. He was in control here and she had better know it. "Well, we are still going to get the land. The methods are going to be different, that's all."

"You are *not* going to get that land! Walt has refused, and by law he can live there as long as he wants to!" Charly was adamant.

Lewis eyed her narrowly for a few moments before saying, "Not if we have him declared mentally incompetent, he can't stay."

Charly's mouth flew open. "Mentally incompetent? But he's *not!*"

"He could be! It wouldn't take much to convince a judge that an eighty-nine-year-old man living far from civilization on government land needs to be in a nursing home. He needs to be watched and cared for! It stands to reason!" He seemed so satisfied with himself.

Charly was furious. "A nursing home? Lewis, you're crazy! I'll never go along with a ridiculous, inhuman plan such as this! Not when Walter Simms doesn't need to be there! I'll fight you all the way!"

"Don't waste your breath, Charly. It won't do any good. If you won't assist, I'll just take you off the project, and you won't have a thing to say about it." Lewis glared at her, his vicious eyes sparking golden daggers in the morning sunlight.

As she looked at him, she realized the extent of his vindictive nature. He was doing this to get back at her! Well, she would fight him!

"Lewis, you can't do this! Walt is . . . is just a nice old man trying to live out his life the way he wants to. He's been there on that mountain for most of his life, and now . . ."

His voice was almost mocking. "Come on, Charly. You're getting soft. What I'm proposing won't hurt him. It'll be better for him in the long haul." Lewis actually believed it. Or did he?

Charly stood and faced Lewis. Her voice was tight as she disclosed painfully, "It'll kill Walt. He'll die if we have him removed from that mountain." She shivered involun-

174

tarily, recalling Noah's exact words to her months ago, when they had discussed removing Walt from the mountain.

It sounded innocent enough. Have him taken care of. It even sounded reasonable and nurturing. Lewis had convinced himself of that. Charly's trouble was that she knew Walt too well. She knew him as a gentle old man who wanted to live out his life on that mountain. Was that too much to ask? *No!*

Lewis jeered laughingly, "He will *not* die, Charly. That's a ridiculous assumption. He will be fine. And he'll be cared for."

Charly flared at him, her face glowing hotly, her voice almost a scream. "Damnit, Lewis, he's 'cared for' now! He's fine—and won't live there forever, you know. Can't you leave him in peace?" Charly was amazed at the sound of her own shrill voice, her staunch defense of the old man on the mountain. What had come over her? She was now opposing the very goal she had once sought! And confronting her boss! She was treading on very thin ice!

Lewis's voice was steely. "I want him off that mountain, now. *Now!*"

Charly spread her hands. "But why? What's the big damn rush?" Should she back off a little?

Instead of answering, Lewis affirmed assertively, "I want him gone, and you're going to sign these papers as the assigned agent. Ben will take care of the project, so you won't have to bother with it anymore."

Charly's head spun with contradictions. Lewis was maneuvering her, forcing her to the culmination—now! His mandate was clearly before her. Still, she urged for reprieve, justice. "Lewis, this is preposterous! The government doesn't do such things!"

His countenance was icy. "I do. And since I'm in charge here, you'll do as I say!" He flung the papers to the table in front of her and flipped a ball-point pen on top.

His words chilled her and she folded her arms to ward off the cold that engulfed her. "I'm not signing anything, Lewis. Certainly not something incriminating toward Walter Simms."

"Sign it, Charly." He muttered through clenched teeth.

She looked down at the papers scattered on the table, then back to Lewis's stone-cold eyes. Suddenly it occurred to Charly that she hated Lewis and everything he was doing. Most particularly, she hated his methods. She decided she would not be commanded by him anymore. Nor would she allow him to intimidate her.

Her brown eyes narrowed coldly at him. "Go to hell, Lewis. You can take your papers and serve them on yourself!" With a surprising amount of calm, she walked to the door.

Just as her hand reached the knob, Lewis barked, "Charly! Get over here. We're not through!"

She held her head high and looked him squarely in the eye. "I am through, Lewis. You won't order me around any longer. I won't be a part of this travesty. I just quit."

Oblivious to the shocked exclamations of both men in the room, Charly closed the door and glided on light feet down the hall to her office. Immediately, she began the mechanics of unloading her desk. It was only a matter of moments before there was a short knock on her door. She glanced up to see Ben—not Lewis, the coward—ease inside.

His voice was gentle, concerned. She was sure he felt somewhat embarrassed to have just witnessed this final confrontation between her and Lewis. "Charly, please, cool down and think about what you just did. You quit a government job, honey. This will ruin your career. Lewis will see to it."

She shook her head. "I don't care. Lewis has lost all of his sense of balance, and I won't be a part of his organization anymore. This whole idea is crazy, you know. What

176

is his reasoning? Or should I say, why has he lost his sense of reason?"

Ben shrugged. "Last year, at one of the national meetings, someone made a comment about the government land being better managed when all the lifetime leases are cleared out. After that, Lewis seemed to take it on himself to eliminate any and all lifetime leases in his district. There was no official proposal, methods were not discussed. Actually, no big deal was made of it. Lewis just decided it would look good on his record. It's an ambitious project."

"Record . . ." Charly seethed. "And Lewis is willing to wreck the remaining few years of a man's life for his own selfish 'record'!"

"Charly, that's not so unusual."

She cocked her head at Ben. "Are you sure it's not personal—because of me? We've never gotten . . . along, and—"

Ben interrupted swiftly. "Naw, Charly. He wouldn't let personal things get in the way of his career."

She nodded sarcastically. "You're probably right. He'd step over any of us . . ."

"Come on, Charly. Talk to Lewis again. Tell him you were upset. Your signature isn't required on this project anyway. He just got carried away. Tell him you—"

Charly's voice rose. "I'm not telling him anything of the sort! You sound as if he's properly brainwashed you, too! I don't care what he does to my career! Nothing is so important as a person's life, and when you lose sight of that, as he has done, you've gone too far!"

"You have lost your perspective, Charly. Save me from your 'hearts and flowers' routine. I've got business to think about! But if what you really wanted to do was to help this old guy, you've blown it. Now you won't have anything to say about the lifetime lease project. You're completely removed from it. You'll regret this move. Mark my words." Shaking his head, he huffed out.

Charly organized her work on the desk and left a few notes here and there. She found some boxes and piled her personal items into them. Within two hours, she was walking into her empty apartment, alone and jobless.

Charly paced the floor and worried—not about her job, but about Walter Simms. All she could think about was Walter and the plan Lewis had for his remaining life. Oddly, Charly was unconcerned about quitting her job and ruining her career. She would worry about that later. She was determined not to regret her actions. Of course, it was too soon to actually be affected by joblessness. However, that was a minor inconvenience compared to the deeper issues.

Charly stopped long enough to fix herself a cheese on rye. She continued her pacing, alternating sips of Coke and bites of sandwich. The fact that plagued her most was what Ben had said before he left her office. If she'd wanted to help Walt, she'd certainly ruined her chances. Now she was in no position . . . or was she?

Walter Simms would be defenseless against Lewis's fiendish strategy. But Noah wasn't. He wasn't defenseless at all. Actually, that's what Noah has been there for all along—to help his friend. Perhaps he could hire a lawyer or . . . something. If he knew about Lewis's plans beforehand, he could block the action . . . somehow. But in order to help Noah had to know about it. And she was the only one who could inform him about Walt's predicament. She would have to be the one.

She sighed heavily and stared out the window. But . . . talk to Noah? Oh, God—how could she? She hadn't seen him, hadn't even heard from him, since that fateful Sunday when she had ordered him out of her life. He had complied with her wishes. Yet they weren't really, *really* her wishes. But what she wanted could never happen. Yes, it was best this way. At least she could handle it.

Oh, she had immediately regretted what she had said to him. She had wanted to call him and apologize. But his disclosure that he didn't love her stopped her from making a fool of herself with him again.

He knew that she loved him. She had admitted it. And he had let her know that the feeling wasn't mutual. So she had decided to forget—to make herself forget—about Noah Van Horn. And she couldn't do that by calling him, apologizing, seeing him occasionally. That would surely break down all her defenses. She had been doing so well these last few lonely months. And now, because of Walter Simms, she would have to risk her emotions by calling him. She bit her lip pensively. But she owed Walter that much. After all, she had given up her job for these principles. She had to do all she possibly could.

So, what's the big deal? Just pick up the phone and call him. Tell him what you know. That's it. He can take it from there.

Boldly, she picked up the phone and dialed the information operator. "North Carolina, please . . . Charlotte . . . Van Horn Furniture Company. . . . Thank you." By the time she had dialed the number, her palms were sweaty and the sandwich she had eaten was in an uncomfortable knot in her stomach. Just the thought of speaking to him was unnerving.

"Hello, Mr. Van Horn, please." Her voice was raspy and she cleared her throat while waiting to be transferred to his office.

She repeated her request to the pleasant-sounding Southern voice who answered. ". . . He's not in? Well, when do you expect him . . . ?" A little disappointment, a little reprieve. ". . . Oh . . . No, I'll get in touch with him later. Thank you."

Damn! He wasn't in and the secretary didn't know when to expect him! And she had worked herself up to talking with him. Her mind reeled. *Oh, why did you have*

179

*to go back up there now? Why can't you stay in your office,
like normal people do?—normal people!*

She paced again. A phone call would have been so easy!
Now what? Charly knew he was on the mountain. She just
felt it. And, she knew there was no way of guessing when
he'd be back to civilization.

Charly busied herself during the afternoon. She cleaned
the kitchen, then straightened the small apartment, threw
a load of clothes in to wash, and went through the boxes
she had brought from her office. She even tossed away
some of the junk that had been there for years and
propped up the inspiring HANG IN THERE plaque someone
had given her. Her eye caught another gift: the rabbit
wood carving *he* had given her. Immediately her mind
raced back to Noah . . . and the mountain . . . and Walter
Simms. She knew what she must do—had known all
along. She had just tried to avoid the inevitable. But she
had to go. With a sigh, she picked up the phone and called
the Atlanta Airport.

The little cabin looked exactly the same as the very first
time she had approached the clearing. She had played it
smart this time and rented a small pickup—a red Datsun
with four-wheel drive. She wouldn't be stranded up here
again! She laughed nervously to herself. Who cared—
now?

She pulled to a stop, got out, and mounted the front
steps, remembering the first time she had arrived at the old
house and how Walt had stood on the porch, watching her
warily. Then he had politely served her lunch.

A chilling wind whistled around the corner of the old
house as she knocked on the door. There was an uneasy,
eerie feeling in the air, and Charly shivered involuntarily.
Receiving no answer, she knocked again, then peered in
through the window. The big room looked the same—
quiet and empty. Then she saw *him*. She caught a glimpse

180

of his dark hair as he sat on the back porch, looking out over the mountains. He didn't respond to her knock, probably couldn't hear her. So she decided to walk around the house.

He slowly turned to face her, when he heard her footsteps on the porch.

"Noah?" Her mouth felt like cotton and she couldn't believe that here she was facing him again. Now what? Hi-how-are-you-and-what-have-you-been-doing-lately? Her dry mouth made further speech impossible for now.

They stared at each other for a moment, Noah obviously shocked to see her, Charly trying to calm her wild heart.

A faint smile crossed his lips as he recognized her. "Charly—what are you doing here?"

After not seeing him for months, she thought he seemed almost bigger than life. He wore jeans and an old blue shirt—the same shirt she had worn in the mountains! His raven-black hair was a little shaggier than when he had been in Atlanta; the dark beard still framed his face boldly. But there was something about his eyes—still beautifully blue, but now red-rimmed and . . . somehow different.

Charly found her voice and tried to sound normal. "I . . . I tried to call you . . . in Charlotte . . . but couldn't get you . . . and I have to talk to you because Lewis is crazy and I have to tell you about what he . . ." She stopped and wondered if she was making any sense at all. Probably not, from the blank expression on his face. But he was nice about it.

"Sit down, Charly." He motioned to the chair next to him, and she sank weakly into it. His hands clenched uneasily, and she remembered those hands on her, around her, caressing her, and she ached to feel them again.

Charly laced her own fingers nervously and tried again. "I told you that I would do what I could to help Walt in this government lease situation. Well, I tried, but it didn't do much good. My boss revived the lifetime-lease project and is determined to get this land. He's going to try to have Walt declared . . . mentally incompetent . . . and I thought you should know." God! It sounded so brutal! She dropped her eyes and tried not to look at his hands. How could she sit so close to him and not touch him—his shoulders . . . his arms . . . his hands.

Noah's expression didn't change as he looked intently at her. She had assumed that he would be as horrified and angry as she was about Lewis's intentions. But he just sat there, as if he were trying to get it all straight in his head. Hadn't she made any sense at all? Finally, after long moments of pressing silence, she rallied. "Noah? Did you hear me? Lewis—"

Noah's upraised hand halted her midsentence. "I heard you." His voice was strangely dull. "But it's too late. Walt's dead."

The words slapped her coldly across the face. "Oh . . . no! Noah—"

Quietly, he answered her unasked questions. "He died two days ago. Heart attack. I rushed him to town, but . . . too late." He spread his strong hands helplessly, looking out into the forest.

Oh, how she wanted to take his hands—to hold him to her breast . . .

Sudden, hot tears burned Charly's eyes. She hardly knew Walter Simms, yet he was responsible for her being sent to the mountain cabin in the first place, for her knowing and subsequently falling in love with Noah, for her quitting her fine, spurious job. And now he was gone.

An empty quiet filled the wintry air, and Charly finally rasped in a hoarse whisper, "I'm sorry, Noah. I . . . I can't believe he's gone. I know he was your friend."

Noah appeared not to notice the two tears that trailed her cheeks. His tone was flat. "He meant a lot to both of us, Charly. At least, what he represented . . ."

"Yes." She smiled in spite of her tears, recalling how

her life, her attitude, even her job had altered since that day when she first drove up the mountain and met the fiesty old man. And Noah. Abruptly, she turned to him, flooded with an empty, sad feeling. "Noah, was all this for nothing? The purpose of everything is changed now that he's gone. The land will automatically revert to the government . . ."

Noah turned to face her, the pain clearly visible in his intense blue eyes. "No, Charly. Everything has a meaning. Especially what has happened between us. I . . . have done a lot of thinking since I left Atlanta. I . . . now realize that I . . . love you. I know this is not the time or the place, but I need to say it. Without you I have been miserable, and I just hope you can forgive me for leaving you."

"Noah—" Charly couldn't believe her ears and slumped against the back of the crude wooden chair.

His hands rubbed his blue-jeaned thighs nervously. "Charly, listen to me. I want you to understand why. You know I've loved you from the start. You must know that. But I just . . . denied it to myself. I . . . I wasn't ready to fall in love—didn't want to—after the death of my wife. I was hurt too much by losing her—them—and my only defense against getting hurt was not to love again. But it happened in spite of me and my denial. With Walt. And with you." Still he didn't look at her, and Charly was going crazy.

She stood and put her hands in his, tugging pleadingly at them. "Noah, I love you, too," she whispered through her tears.

He looked up at her, painfully, questioningly. "Can you forgive me, Charly?" Immediately, he was on his feet, cupping her face with his sensitive hands. His kiss was gentle, loving, longed for . . . "I love you, Charly. I love you . . ." His words were lost against her tear-stained face. He wrapped his long arms around her, enfolding her with his love and warmth. She buried her face against his chest, savoring the closeness, his fragrance, his caress. Somehow she knew they would never part again.

They stood together for a long time, holding each other, drawing strength and love. They reveled in the admissions of love that were finally out in the open—revealed to each other and the world.

Finally, reluctantly, Noah sighed and pushed away from their embrace. "Charly, I have some unfinished business. Will you help me?"

"What?" Charly noticed the strained expression on his face.

"I promised Walt not to leave any traces of his habitation here on this mountain." He motioned toward two large gasoline cans near the door.

"Burn it?" Charly asked, alarmed.

He nodded silently and bent to lift one of the full cans.

"Noah! You can't!" She grabbed his arm.

He looked at her fiercely and she knew immediately that he would. "I've packed my books and things. What's left was Walt's and he wanted it all destroyed. I promised him." He went inside and she could hear him splashing the flammable liquid against the walls.

Without thinking, she grabbed the other can and helped Noah douse the place with the smelly stuff. Somehow it struck her as humorous. "You know, if I hadn't already quit my job, this would certainly do it up for me. My career ruined. Arson of government property isn't exactly smiled upon by authorities!" She smiled at the thought of Lewis's face if he knew.

Noah emptied his can and tossed it into the kitchen. "Quit your job? When? Why?"

They left the house together, and Charly shrugged. "Lewis and I had one final confrontation—over this lifetime-lease project. I just couldn't go along with him anymore. His latest strategy was the last straw, as Walt would say. I couldn't let him do that to Walt."

184

"Charly, I can't believe you gave up your job over this . . . this situation."

"Why?"

"Well, it meant so much to you, for one thing." He fished in his pocket for matches.

"I have discovered that people are more important than jobs." She smiled. Reaching up, she pulled his face toward her, kissing him, loving the feeling of his lips and beard.

He smiled devilishly at her. "So the world's greatest sculptress has quit her job? Afraid of the heights, huh? Well, you're in luck, because I'm hiring for the world's greatest lover position."

"You are?" She giggled, remembering their jokes in happier times. "Can I apply? I do need a job."

"Sure. But I require strict loyalty. A lifetime of it. Accompanied by a marriage certificate. Those not qualified need not apply."

"Marriage?"

He kissed her ear and said softly, "You're highly qualified, Wildcat."

"Noah—" She drew back. "Did you mean . . . married . . . us?"

"Of course. How else will I test your loyalty? Are you interested in the position?"

"Yes—oh, yes! I'm definitely interested!" She grabbed him fiercely around the neck and hugged with all her might. He was hers to love forever!

Patiently, he removed her arms from their clutch around him. "Charly, I have a job to finish. Move your car back to safety and I'll light this." His voice was grim. "We'll have to make sure it doesn't spread, so we can't leave until it's gone."

Charly nodded solemnly, containing her happiness until the unpleasant business before them was completed. She moved the rented truck to the far edge of the clearing, away from the house, and was soon joined by Noah. Within minutes the small wooden cabin seemed to explode into flames. It crackled loudly as the huge tower of reddish-yellow flames rose high in the sky, engulfing the walls and roof. Suddenly a wall of choking grief rose in Charly and flowed from her in deep, racking sobs. She turned to Noah, who embraced her, comforting, murmuring softly. She cried until there were no more tears, and when she lifted her head from his chest the little cabin was nearly gone.

"It's all right, Charly. It's what he wanted." Noah's voice was firm now.

"I . . . I know," she agreed. "It's just that . . ." She halted and smiled sheepishly through her tears. "This is where we first made love and . . . I know I'm a sentimental fool." She sniffed and tried to laugh.

"Maybe. But I love you that way, Charly." His hand traveled gently from her shoulder to caress her neck. "The cabin can be destroyed, but, like the diamonds, our love will last forever."

She smiled happily and saw her reflection in his blue eyes.

"Let's go home, Charly." He kissed her again, a tender reminder of their forever love.

Once you've tasted joy and passion, do you dare dream of

LOVING

Danielle Steel

bestselling author of
The Promise and *To Love Again*

Bettina Daniels lived in a gilded world—pampered, adored, adoring. She had youth, beauty and a glamorous life that circled the globe—everything her father's love, fame and money could buy. Suddenly, Justin Daniels was gone. Bettina stood alone before a mountain of debts and a world of strangers—men who promised her many things, who tempted her with words of love. But Bettina had to live her own life, seize her own dreams and take her own chances. But could she pay the bittersweet price?

A Dell Book ═══════════════════ $3.50 (14684-4)

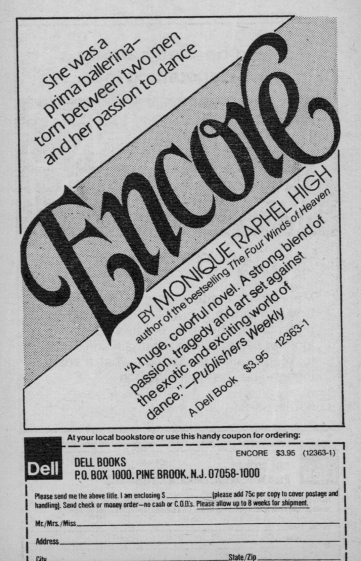

A cold-hearted bargain...
An all-consuming love...

THE TIGER'S WOMAN

by Celeste De Blasis
bestselling author of *The Proud Breed*

Mary Smith made a bargain with Jason
Drake, the man they called The Tiger: his
protection for her love, his strength to protect her secret. It was a bargain she swore
to keep...until she learned what it really
meant to be The Tiger's Woman.

A Dell Book $3.95   11820-4
